WHILE
DROWNING
IN THE
DESERT

Also by Don Winslow

WHILE DROWNING IN THE DESERT

A Neal Carey Mystery
by Don Winslow

St. Martin's Press ❧ New York

Design by Scott Levine

Library of Congress Cataloging-in-Publication Data

Winslow, Don
    While drowning in the desert : a Neal Carey mystery / by Don
Winslow. — 1st ed.
        p.   cm.
    ISBN 0-312-14446-6
    1. Carey, Neal (Fictitious character)—Fiction.   2. Comedians—
Nevada—Las Vegas—Fiction.   3. Bodyguards—California—Fiction.
I. Title.
PS3573.I5326W48   1996   ℏ 34046772
813'.54—dc20   96-1249
                                                            CIP

First Edition: June 1996

10 9 8 7 6 5 4 3 2 1

In memory of my father, Don Winslow, who taught me—among so many other things—how to look at life and laugh.

Acknowledgments

Thanks to Ric Ericson, Richard Sabellico, and the cast of "Little Rhody's Big Burlesque" for the education.

WHILE DROWNING IN THE DESERT

Prologue

I NEVER SHOULD HAVE GOT OUT OF THE HOT TUB.

I was luxuriating in the steaming water when Karen asked me to get her a Diet Pepsi.

"Excuse me?" I murmured.

"I'm in postcoital bliss," she said. "And when I'm in postcoital bliss I need a Diet Pepsi."

"Why don't you get one?"

She shook her head.

"When a woman's in postcoital bliss it's the guy's job to get the Diet Pepsi," she smiled. "It's a rule."

"I'm in postcoital bliss, too."

"Too bad."

I saw I wasn't going to win so I lifted myself out of the tub. She looked at me with what I wanted to think was a lascivious expression.

"Besides," she said, "it's your fault."

That was very nice of her to say.

"Then you don't mind if I get myself one, too?" I asked.

"Not at all."

Even though no one could see us on the deck of our house I wrapped a towel around my midriff as I padded into the kitchen. I turned to admire Karen as she stretched her long neck back onto the edge of the tub and closed her eyes. Her black hair was wet with steam. Her wide mouth bent into a smile.

I loved her to distraction.

I had just opened the refrigerator and taken out two cold, shiny cans of Diet Pepsi when the phone rang.

And stopped.

I stood stock-still and watched the sweep hand on the kitchen clock. No, no, no, no, I thought. Let it be a wrong number. Let it be an obscene caller that chickened out. But don't let it ring again in thirty seconds.

Exactly thirty seconds later it rang again.

I snatched the receiver off the hook and snapped, "What."

I knew who it was.

"Son!" Graham's mock cheerful voice pierced my eardrum.

And it had been such a nice evening.

"Hello, Dad," I moaned.

"Dad" was not actually my father in the biological sense. We met when I was twelve years old and tried to pick his pocket in a bar. He pretty much raised me after that, even to the extent of teaching me a trade.

The trade he taught me included such skills as breaking and entering, following people, stealing documents from offices, searching hotel rooms, and finding the lost, missing, and running.

In short, he taught me how to be a private eye.

Like him.

"You don't sound happy to hear from me!"

I could picture him on the other end of the line, sitting in his immaculate Murray Hill apartment, his artificial right arm set at a kitchen table that Christian Barnaard could operate on. I could imagine his cherubic little face, his thin, sandy hair greased straight back, and his aggravating, satanic grin.

"Not exactly."

I know, I know. Petulant and rude. But a phone call that starts in code is not going to be good news. The single ring and thirty-second gap meant that this wasn't a social call, but business.

And I didn't want to get back to business.

Graham said, "My feelings are hurt."

"Yeah, right."

The Giants blowing the point spread with twelve seconds to play, *that* might hurt Graham's feelings.

"How are the wedding plans coming?" he asked politely.

Wedding *plans*? I thought in a moment of alarm. What

was there to plan? I figured that everyone would show up at the Milkovsky ranch, and Karen and I would say the *I do*'s, and that would be about it.

"Uhh, fine," I answered.

"Have you registered your patterns?"

"Uhhh, yeah."

Registered? Patterns?

"What about the honeymoon?"

"In favor of it."

"Great vacations don't just happen, you know," Graham said.

I had never thought of a honeymoon as precisely a vacation, but I let it pass. Instead I said, "You didn't call me just to nag me about wedding plans."

"No, that's just a bonus. We have a little job for you."

"I thought I was on permanent disability," I said. Ed Levine, our mutual boss at Friends of the Family, had officially declared me mentally ill. I knew Ed didn't really think that I was actually crazy, just that I drove *him* nuts. Either way, it worked for me.

By the way, my name is Neal Carey. I don't carry a badge.

Actually I never did. Even in the days when I was working I didn't have a badge. Or a license or a gun or any of that private eye stuff. I just did the stuff that Friends asked me to do, and if that isn't crazy. . . .

"We decided that you've recovered," Graham announced.

"No, I'm still crazy."

4

"Don't get your panties all wet," Graham said. "It's a short job. In fact, let's not even call it a job. Let's call it a errand."

"What kind of 'a errand'?"

Because this was no time for a job *or* an errand. Not only was I getting married in two months, I was also heading into the last semester of my master's program at Nevada. I even had my thesis, *Tobias Smollett and the Image of the Outsider in Eighteenth-Century English Literature,* almost finished. Dr. Baskin, my old professor at Columbia, thought he could get me an assistantship in the Ph.D. program there, and Karen was cool about going to New York for a couple of years. So this was no time to get involved in some wacko job for Friends.

And Friends has some wacko jobs, all right. Friends of the Family is a confidential service that "The Bank" in Providence, Rhode Island, provides for its wealthier depositors. I had worked on and off for Friends since the day Graham found my hand in his back pocket.

Graham said, "This old guy wandered away from his home and ended up in Las Vegas. His niece has a couple of million in The Bank and is worried sick about him. Thinks maybe he has Alzheimer's or something. She's a friend of the family. We were wondering, what with you being so close, if you'd pick him up and take him home."

If I haven't mentioned it, Karen and I lived in Austin, Nevada, a small, remote town in the Toiyabe mountain range. It's six hours and a hundred years away from Las Vegas.

"I'm supposed to find him in Vegas?"

"You don't even have to find him," Graham answered. "He's in a nice room at the Mirage and security's keeping an eye on him. It's a no-brainer, which is why I thought of you."

There has to be a catch, I thought.

"Where does he live? Tibet?"

"Palm Desert."

"Where's that?"

"Next to Palm Springs."

"California?"

"No. Palm Springs, Antarctica."

Graham has a gift for sarcasm.

A pause, then Graham repeated, "Alone and confused. An old man."

He also has a gift for bathos. *Bathos* is one of those graduate-school words you don't often get a chance to trot out. Bathos, bathos, bathos.

"All right, all right," I said.

"You'll do it?"

"I'm a sucker."

Especially for bathos.

"Nathan Silverstein," Graham said. "Room 5812. He's expecting you, but clear it through security first, right?"

"Right."

"Now, what am I supposed to wear?" Graham asked. "I hope this isn't going to be one of those blue-jeans weddings."

"See you, Dad."

"Bye-bye, son."

I hung up and grabbed the sodas. This wasn't so bad after all. I'd be gone a couple of days and pick up a few extra bucks. And not get dragged back into Friends.

Yep, master's degree soon, deliriously happy marriage, back to New York for a while. I had life pretty much wired. And maybe Karen had evolved into some *pre*coital bliss in my extended absence.

When I got back outside she was sobbing.

"Honey, what's the matt—"

She looked at me with red-rimmed eyes and bawled, "I want a baaaaby!"

I never should have got out of the hot tub.

Chapter 1

A BABY, I THOUGHT THE NEXT MORNING AS I drove the Jeep down lonely Highway 93 toward Las Vegas. A baby, I thought, replaying the whole argument.

"We're not even married yet," I'd said to Karen as we sat on the edge of the hot tub.

"We will be in two months," she answered.

We'd decided on an early-October wedding out at the ranch of our best friends, the Milkovskys.

I trotted out some old cliché I'd seen on a talk show. "But I thought we'd have some time together just as a couple before we brought a third person into it."

"We've been living together for almost two years," she reminded me. Then she got pissed off. "And how dare you speak of our baby as 'a third person'?"

It had sounded so good on television, too.

"The damn thing's not even born yet," I muttered.

Mistake.

" 'The damn thing'?! The *'damn thing'?*"

"You know what I meant."

She looked at me accusingly. "You don't want a baby."

"Yes I do."

"No you don't."

"I do," I answered. "Just not *right now.*"

"When?"

"What, you want a *date?*"

"Yes, a date."

I thought about it for a second, then said, "In two years."

"Two *years?!*" she screeched. "Neal, I've been getting weepy over McDonald's commercials!"

"Maybe it's just one of those hormonal things," I said.

That did it. She got up and stomped into the house before I could say, "And then maybe again it isn't."

So early the next morning when I said, "Karen, honey, I'm leaving," she just said, "Good."

"I'll be back in a couple of days."

"Yippee."

"Uhh, can I bring you anything?"

"Sperm."

Sperm, I thought as I reached Vegas' northern burbs. I've become *sperm.* Sperm leads to babies. Which leads to diapers and rashes and colic and to a *person,* which was the scariest thing of all because a little person expects things from you. Daddy-type things.

The problem is, I have no experience with this stuff.

No role model, as it were, my own father having been your classic anonymous sperm donor who knocked up my prostitute mother. No role model unless you count Joe Graham, the one-armed dwarf of a private eye who raised me, taught me a trade, and set me up with Friends of the Family.

A *father.*

I don't know.

> > >

I was still thinking this over—and developing a wicked headache—when I gave the Jeep to the valets at the Mirage and found my way to the security desk in the basement.

"Hi," I said to the thickly muscled, blue-blazered man behind the counter. I slid my wallet—open to show my driver's license—over the counter. "I'm Neal Carey. I'm here to escort Mr. Silverstein home."

"Natty Silver," the guard said, chuckling.

"You know him?"

"You don't?"

"Sorry."

"Natty Silver!" the guard prompted. "One of the great burlesque top bananas. When that died he went stand-up. Worked this town when it was just the Flamingo. You probably saw him on *Ed Sullivan.*"

"*That* Natty Silver?!" I vaguely remembered the

comic's baggy checked pants and deadpan delivery.

" 'Wherever you go, there you are,' Natty Silver?"

"The one and only."

"Whatever happened to him?"

"Ah, he did some more stand-up, a few shitty beach movies where the kids made fun of him. He faded. Christ, he must be, what, eighty-six, eight-seven?"

"Natty Silver," I repeated.

"I'll call up, let him know you're coming," the guard said.

Natty Silver, I thought. This might be kind of fun. Uh-huh.

❭ ❭ ❭

I rang the doorbell to room 5812.

"Who is it?" a voice asked from behind the door.

"Mr. Silverstein, it's me. Neal Carey."

"Am I expecting you?"

"Yes, you are."

My head throbbed.

"Where are you from, Neal Carey?"

"Originally, New York."

A long pause.

"City or state?" the voice asked.

Throb, throb, throb.

"City," I answered.

Pause.

"East or West Side?"

"West."

Another long pause, during which the throbbing turned to pounding.

"Mr. Silverstein?" I asked. "Are you okay?"

"Who's buried in Grant's Tomb?"

A trick question.

"Grant and *Mrs.* Grant," I said. You have to get up pretty early in the afternoon to put one over on Neal Carey.

"What's on the corner of Fifty-eighth and Amsterdam?" he asked.

"There *is* no corner of Fifty-eighth and Amsterdam."

Who did he think he was playing with, a child? I thought with some annoyance. Of course, if I hadn't been so annoyed, I might have asked myself the question: Why is Nathan Silverstein being so careful and what is he afraid of? But I was too concerned with my own state of mind to think of that. This is what happens when you tend to be as self-absorbed as I am.

The door opened a sliver. I saw a tiny face with big blue eyes peek out.

Great, I thought. My fiancée wants an insta-child and I end up babysitting Yoda.

"Hi," I said.

Okay, okay. I never claimed to be a great wit.

"Hello yourself."

"May I come in?"

"Why not?"

12

Nathan Silverstein was a small man with wispy white hair, a small beak of a nose, and skin as crinkled and tan as an old paper bag. He was wearing a white terrycloth robe with *Mirage* stenciled on it and a pair of cloth slippers.

"Say, didn't I meet you in Cleveland once?" he asked me.

"I've never been to Cleveland."

"Neither have I," Silverstein said. "Must have been two other guys."

Yeah, that's me: straight man to the universe.

"You wouldn't have any aspirin, would you?" I asked.

Chapter 2

". . . SO THE GUYS SAYS, 'I DON'T KNOW. I NEVER LIT it!' "

Nat Silver gave the old punch line and looked at me expectantly.

I laughed politely and said, "Mr. Silverstein, I'm here to escort you home."

"You're an escort service?" Silver asked. "The last time I called an escort service I got a young honey with big bazookas. I mean, you're a good-looking kid, but . . ."

"How did you get here, Mr. Silverstein?"

"Everybody's got to be someplace," Silverstein shrugged. Then he added, "Wherever you go, there you are."

"Yeah, but to Vegas . . ."

"Here's your aspirin."

"Thanks."

"You want to go see the tigers?" Silverstein asked. "They got tigers here."

"No thanks."

"*White* tigers."

I don't care if they're *plaid*, I thought. We need to get to the airport.

"We have a four-o'clock flight to Palm Springs," I said.

Nathan frowned and shuffled over to a chair in the corner of the room. He let himself down slowly and stared at the floor.

He looked pathetic.

Nathan Silverstein was in his mid-eighties, at least. He was frail, of course, with his few strands of wispy white hair and the translucent skin of the elderly, but he had the eyes of an eight-year-old in a candy store.

Now the eyes were staring at the floor trying hard to look . . . pathetic.

"Are you okay, Mr. Silverstein?" I asked.

"I'm old," Nathan answered.

What could I say?

"You're only as old as you feel," I said.

It was the best I could think of. Give me a break.

"I *feel* old," Nathan said. He took a pack of Winstons from the side table, slipped a cigarette into his mouth, and shook the lighter toward his lips.

"This is a non-smoking room," I observed.

"The room isn't smoking," Nate snapped. "*I'm* smoking. If the room was smoking, I'd leave the room. I may be old, I'm not an idiot."

"Okay."

Nate inhaled, then coughed for about ten seconds. Inhaled, coughed. Inhaled, coughed. Then he said, "Let's go get a drink. I'm thirsty."

"Our flight doesn't leave for three hours," I said.

"Good," Nate said. "I'm horny, too."

> > >

I watched television while Nate dressed. Or I tried to, anyway, because Nate kept up a nonstop monologue from the bathroom.

"Eighty-six-year-old Mr. Birnbaum goes to confession," Nate said. "Says, 'Father, last night I had sex with a twenty-year-old girl.' Priest says, 'Mr. Birnbaum, you're Jewish, why are you telling me?' Birnbaum says, 'Father, I'm telling *everybody*.'

"Birnbaum checks into a hotel with the girl. Desk clerk says, 'Birnbaum, aren't you afraid of a heart attack?' Birnbaum says, 'If she dies, she dies!'

"Mrs. Birnbaum comes home one day and finds him in bed with a girl. She throws him out the window. Cop comes and asks, 'Why did you throw your husband out the window?' She says, 'I thought if he could *schtupp*, he could fly.'

"Crowd gathers on the street where Birnbaum fell. Another cop pushes through the crowd and asks Birnbaum what happened. Birnbaum says, 'I don't know, I just got here myself.' "

I knew just how Birnbaum felt. *I* was beginning to look for a window. Of course the windows in Vegas hotels don't actually open, which is a pretty good idea when you think about it. You'd need a three-digit over/under on the daily number of competitors in the 100 Meter Concrete Diving Competition. And you'd still get some guy taking the million-to-one odds that this time, this *one* time, some poor suicidal loser is going to step out the window and fall *up*.

You give big enough odds, you'll find a dreamer in this town to take them. A thousand-to-one that tomorrow's Washington *Post* will feature a picture of Elvis and Ronald Reagan secretly worshipping a bust of Leon Trotsky in the laundry room of The White House? Done. Two-million-to-one that Mother Teresa will spend the night in the slammer after a barroom brawl in Passaic, New Jersey? Done. Five-trillion-to-one that a Rhode Island transportation official will issue a highway construction contract without taking a kickback . . .

Well, okay, there are some things no one would bet on.

When Nate emerged from the bathroom he was wearing white shoes, plaid trousers, a canary yellow shirt and a white golf hat.

"Funeral?" I asked.

"Why do you think they call me Natty?" Nate asked. He picked up his cane and asked, "So are we going or what?"

"We're going," I said.

It took a while to get to the bar. Not because the elevator was slow or the floor was particularly crowded but because Nate took the time to ogle each cocktail waitress that crossed within a fifty-foot radius of his immediate gaze.

Actually, it wasn't so much an ogle as much it was a long, leisurely evaluation that started at the targeted woman's feet and slowly progressed to the top of her head. Nate's gaze started with a concentrated frown and ended with an appreciative smile. Nor was Nate the least bit surreptitious about it—he stared at these women with the unself-conscious glare of a judge in the bathing-suit competition at a beauty contest. It was the kind of look that would get the average man a subpoena.

But the objects of Nate's attention just looked at his cute little avian face and smiled. One of those "Isn't he cute?" smiles. They didn't realize that while the old man was undressing them with his eyes he was undressing himself at the same time.

I figured that Nate had gotten laid in his own mind at least fifty times by the time we finally made it to the lounge.

Nate insisted on sitting at the bar, so I helped him get up on a stool and sat in constant readiness to catch him.

"Mr. Silver," the bartender said. "The usual?"

The *usual*?

"And whatever my friend here is having," Nate said.

"A gin and tonic, please."

I reached for my wallet but Nate hastily said, "Put it on my tab."

The bartender set the drinks down and looked expectantly at Nate. Nate took a sip of his vodka collins, leaned over the bar, and asked, "Have you seen Jayne Mansfield's new shoes?"

The bartender grinned like someone left a twenty-dollar tip and said that he hadn't.

"Neither has she," Nate said.

The bartender guffawed, shook his head, and I thought, *Jayne Mansfield?* I was trying to remember how many decades it had been since Jayne Mansfield died when Nate looked at me and said sadly, "I was with the same woman for fifty years."

"Wow," I said. This was about to get bathetic.

"Then my wife found out."

Nate turned on the stool to get a better view of the women playing the slot machines and damn near fell off trying to get a closer view of the wide albeit heart-shaped rear end of a peroxide blonde who was bending over to collect her quarters. She looked over her shoulder, saw him staring, and gave him a real hard look.

This was trouble.

The woman straightened up and stepped over to the bar. She was about five-ten and wore a tight, white, sequined evening dress with a push-up bra that could only have been designed with Atlas in mind. Her high heels showed off long legs leading to generous hips. I figured her to be somewhere between forty-eight and sixty-eight under the makeup. She had a sweet, pretty face and deep cornflower blue eyes.

Which were staring right at Natty.

I was formulating apologies when the woman squealed, *"Natty?!"*

"Hope?" Natty asked. "I thought that was you, darling. Who else has a tush like that?"

I was waiting to see Nate's head go flying off his skinny neck when Hope smiled and said, "You always knew how to sweet-talk a lady, Natty Silver."

She threw her arms around him and Natty disappeared into a cloud of breasts and big hair. I was afraid Natty would suffocate but Natty emerged a few seconds later a bit red-faced but with a rake's smile spread all over his little face.

"Hope," he said, "meet my friend . . ."

He didn't have a clue.

"Neal Carey," I said.

"Nice to meet you, Neal."

"A cocktail, Hope?" Nate asked.

"Let me go freshen my face first," Hope said.

Nate watched her sashay across the floor, then fumbled in his pocket for his wallet. He took it out, found a twenty-dollar bill, handed it to me and said, "Go take in a movie, kid."

"Huh?"

"Or play the slots or something."

Nathan winked.

"Huh?" I asked again.

"What, I gotta draw you a picture?"

It took a moment for it to sink in and then I said, "You're kidding, right?"

And I definitely didn't want a see a picture.

Nate looked genuinely offended.

"What?" he asked. "You think that because there's snow on the roof, there's no fire in the oven?"

"Mr. Silverstein, we have a—"

"I'll spell it out for you: Get lost."

"—plane to catch, and—"

"Beat it."

"—I have to get you back to Palm Desert."

"I still have the *room!*" Nate whispered urgently, because Hope was hip-switching back to the bar.

"And don't you look lovely," Nate said as Hope slid onto the stool next to him.

"I have to make a quick phone call," I said.

"Take your time," said Nate.

"Nice to meet you," said Hope. "A Bloody Mary, please."

I found a phone from where I could still keep an eye on Nate and Hope and dialed home.

Karen's probably over this baby thing by now, I thought. Probably just a bad case of hormones.

Karen answered on the third ring.

"Hi," I said.

"Hi."

Her voice was as warm as a January morning in Chicago.

"How are you?" I asked.

"Not pregnant."

And hung up.

I stood pretending to be listening, then hung up and walked back to the bar to rescue Hope.

"Who did you call?" Natty muttered. "Time and temperature?"

Then he turned back to Hope.

"Well," I said, "it's probably about time to check out and head for the airport."

They weren't listening.

"Nice lounge," Nate said.

"Very pleasant," answered Hope.

"A little noisy, though," Nate said.

Oh, God.

"Hard to conduct a conversation," Hope agreed.

Nate said, "I wish there were a quiet place we could have a nice chat."

"That would be lovely."

I watched as Nate feigned deep thought, then said, "I have an idea!"

I'll bet you do.

"We could go up to my room," Nate suggested.

Surprise, surprise.

"By the time we check out," I said, "park . . ."

"*Room* service," Nate said.

". . . get our boarding passes . . ."

"A little drink, a little chat . . ." Nate said. "Talk over old times. Nothing *you'd* be interested in, Neal."

Hope looked over Natty's shoulder and gave me a look. One of those significant looks. A "Help me" look.

"You just can't get to the airport too early these days," I said.

"Or you can always catch a later flight," said Nate.

Hope slid off the stool and said, "Could I have a word with you, Neal? Alone?"

She took him me the elbow and guided me a few steps away.

I smiled and whispered, "Look, I know. Why don't you make your excuse, I'll get him on his plane and—"

She dug into her purse, doubtless searching for her car keys. "Neal, sweetie," she said, pressing a twenty into my palm, "can I treat you to a movie or something?"

I slipped the bill back to her.

"Save your money."

She looked at me with those big blue eyes.

She must have been something, I thought. In fact, she was not at all unattractive now. And there were still a couple of hours before the flight, the airport was close and I could still get Nathan back to Palm Desert tonight.

"You know how it is," she said.

Yeah, I thought. I was young once myself.

Chapter 3

LAS VEGAS IS THE WEIRDEST PLACE IN THE world.

I've been to some pretty weird places. Hell, I grew up—or failed to, depending on your perspective—in New York City. Weird. I've worked cases in San Francisco (weird), London (weird) and Hollywood (very weird). I even spent three years as a prisoner of sorts in a Buddhist monastery in the remote mountains of western Sichuan in China (very, very weird).

But on the general scale of weird, Las Vegas has all these places beat hands-down, so to speak.

I think it's what happens when you have a combination of unlimited space and unlimited money unconstrained by common sense or good taste. Things can get pretty weird.

I mean here in a state run by Mormons you have a town

founded by a Jewish gangster whose nickname was Bugsy. He gets the weird ball rolling when he builds the first casino and calls it what? The Flamingo.

In a desert.

A big pink bird that lives in the water.

In Africa.

I don't know about you, but if I'm standing in the middle of a Nevada desert, one of the first things I think of is *not* an African bird that stands around with one leg in the water.

But, then again, the guy's nickname was Bugsy, right?

So Bugsy built the Flamingo, came in way over budget and got a Mafia pink slip. After the funeral, a couple of other boys built casinos with names like the Sands (not weird), the Oasis (not weird), and the Sahara (confused, but not weird) but that's where the non-weirdness stopped.

Because people started coming to Las Vegas.

To do what?

Lose money.

It became one of the great American pastimes. Save your money all year to go on vacation and lose the money. People started treating it as if it were some sort of wonderfully guilty pleasure. *Yeah, I went to Vegas last week and really lost my shirt. Heh-heh-heh.*

The gangsters couldn't believe it. Here they'd spent all those years of effort and planning on *crime* and it all suddenly seemed like such a waste. Now all they had to do was build a bunch of hotel rooms, tell people they could stay in them for twenty bucks if they promised to lose five hundred at the tables, and people actually went for it. *Yeah, I went to Vegas last week and dropped two grand. But guess what? My room? Twenty bucks. And the buffets . . .*

Mob-organized bank robberies stopped virtually overnight. Why go to all the trouble and danger of robbing a bank when all you had to do was invite the bank to come to Las Vegas? And the beauty of it: it was all perfectly legal.

Anyway, the money kept coming in and the casinos kept going up and the weirdness quotient kept rising.

To the point where you could now walk, as I was doing that Sunday afternoon, from a casino where they have a mock volcanic eruption every two hours, to a pirate ship, to ancient Rome, to a paddle-wheeled steamboat, to a Chinese temple, to a circus where they have acrobats flying around over your head while you're trying to drop twenty bucks' worth of quarters into a slot machine while some waitress dressed like a lion tamer offers you free drinks.

Weird.

Not that I was gambling. I wasn't. In the first place I don't like gambling and in the second place I was too busy looking for Natty Silver and dreading the phone call I had to make.

I finally pulled my sorry ass into a phone booth and made the call.

"So how's Palm Springs?" Graham asked.

"Uhhh," I answered, "it's a nice town."

There was a long pause.

"You're not there, are you?" Graham asked.

"Uhhh, yes," I said.

"Yes, you're there?"

"Yes, I'm *not* there."

I don't have any bananas, either.

Another silence.

"How's Silverstein?" Graham asked.

"Funny," I said. "He's a funny old guy."

A sigh of resignation then, "He's not there, is he?"

"No."

"Where is he?"

"That's sort of the question of the hour, Dad."

I hated saying it. Hated explaining it to Graham. Hated the sound of the words as they came out of my mouth. But it was the truth.

I'd given Nathan and Hope an hour and when I went back to the room no one answered. I ran down to the lounge, checked it and several other lounges, ran through the gaming tables, the slot machines, the sports room, the pool complex and then thought of the white tigers exhibit.

They weren't there, either. Oh, the white tigers were there, just no sign of Nathan or Hope.

"How do you lose an eighty-six-year-old man?!" Graham yelled. "What did he do, Neal, outrun you? Cold-cock you with his cane? Gum you into unconsciousness?"

"He got out of my sight, I guess."

Graham screeched, "Why did you let him get out of your sight?!"

So he could get laid or whatever, I thought. But I was too embarrassed to say it so I settled for, "We bumped into an old friend of his and they took off together for a few minutes."

"Who was the old friend? Mother Teresa?" Graham asked. "She outrun you too?"

"Some of those nuns are pretty fast, Graham."

Some of them are, too. Especially with a ruler in their hands.

Graham asked, "Who was the friend?"

"A woman."

Sigh. "Name?"

"Hope."

"Last name?"

"Dunno."

"So, can you find him?" Graham asked.

"Dad, the way he's dressed, Stevie Wonder could find him."

"Stevie Wonder's blind—"

"Yeah . . ."

"—he's not a moron!"

Click.

I went back to the bar. In the first bit of good luck I'd had since I got out of the hot tub the same bartender was on duty.

"The woman who was sitting here with me and Natty Silver?" I said.

"Yeah?"

"Do you know her name?"

"Yes I do."

My headache started to come back.

"What is her name?" I asked.

"Hope."

"Does Hope have a last name?"

"Yes, she does."

"Do you know what it is?"

"Yes, I do."

What have I done? I thought. What have I done to deserve all these little torments?

I decided that it was some sort of cosmic female conspiracy—that was it. Let a basically decent guy hesitate for the slightest second to instantly impregnate his fiancée, on her slightest whim, and the whole universe starts messing with him.

"What is her last name?" I asked.

"Her last name is White."

"What do you know about her?"

"Lots."

"Listen," I said, "I'm just trying to help Mr. Silverstein."

The bartender chuckled.

"Looked like he was doing all right by himself," the bartender said. "Besides, you're not his buddy. You were laughing at him."

"You were laughing at him, too."

"I was *laughing* at him," the bartender said. "You were laughing *at* him."

I thought about it for a second then said, "Yeah, you're right."

"Yes, I am."

I got up from the stool. "Thanks for the name."

"Hope White," the bartender said, "used to be a chorus girl. Worked all the big shows. When gravity took its toll she switched to cocktail-bar piano. She's good enough to work the morning shift in the older casinos. You know, Cole Porter tunes to guys with hangovers waiting for a table in the breakfast buffets. I think maybe now she's at the Nugget. She gets off, she plays the slots. Nice lady. That's Hope White."

"Thanks."

"Thanks for saying thanks."

And thanks for reminding me what a total asshole I can be.

)　　)　　)

Like Hope White and Natty Silver, the Nugget had seen better days. And like Hope White and Natty Silver, it wasn't going down without a few laughs.

The walls were dingy, the carpets worn. The tables had seen more than their share of winning and lots more than anyone's share of losing. The clientele were blue-collar workers on an economy vacation, or local seniors on a fixed budget, or those few sad high-rollers for whom a string of sevens was a distant memory of something that never happened. The casino smelled of stale smoke, old booze and drugstore perfume.

I found the piano bar. A middle-aged woman with dyed

red hair sat at the keys, trying to stretch "I Get a Kick Out of You" into ten minutes. She was doing pretty well at it, too. I took a seat at the piano and put a five in the glass.

When she wound up the tune she said, "You're a little young for this place, honey."

"I'm looking for Hope White."

The redhead smiled. "You're a little young for her place, too."

"I'm throwing a birthday party for my mother," I explained. "I want to see if I can hire Miss White to come play."

"She's eight to noon, sweetie."

"And I work."

"I got her number."

The redhead dug around in her purse and handed me two cards, one of Hope White's and one of her own.

"If Hope can't do it," she explained.

"You'll be the first I call," I said. "Thanks."

I looked at Hope's card. It read, *The Great Hope White. Cocktail Chanteuse Extraordinaire.*

The Great Hope White. Pretty funny.

> > >

"Hi," I said when Hope answered the door of her old bungalow in Vegas' declining old section. "Can Nathan come out and play?"

Hope was wrapped in an unbelted white robe probably designed by Omar the Tentmaker.

"Nathan's not here," she said.

"Would you like to come in?" Hope asked me.

Without waiting for an answer she took my shoulder and guided me past her into the living room. Her perfume smelled liked gardenias—lots of them.

Going from the hot dry air outside into her house was like stepping from a desert into a jungle. It was actually humid in there. Fetid, one might say if one said graduate school words like 'fetid' and 'bathos.' If, indeed, one said words like "one" when referring to oneself.

Anyway, it was hot and humid and chock–full of plants, which was a relief to me. I was afraid it was going to be cats. But it was plants and they were everywhere. Not cactuses either (yes, I know it's "cacti," but I've already used "fetid", "bathos" and "one", and even *I* have a limit on being pretentious.) No, these were leafy green plants of the kind I regularly killed when I had an apartment in New York, and they were all dripping with moisture. It looked like she watered them maybe fifteen times a day. I half-expected an alligator to come running out from behind one of them.

"My babies," she explained.

"You must have a green thumb," I answered.

Back to the lack of wit thing.

She motioned for me to sit and I plopped down on an orange sofa that looked around vintage 1965. There was a glass coffee table, a television set, two other chairs from the Johnson administration, and two or three hundred framed photographs.

The photographs occupied virtually every inch of space that wasn't being taken up by organic matter. There were photos on the walls, on the coffee table, on several little side tables that seemed to exist for the purpose, and on the television set.

Most of the photos were pictures of Hope with people. Some were celebrities—I recognized Sinatra, Tony Bennett, and Wayne Newton—and some of them seemed to be entertainers whose names had never made it above the title. Judging from their placement it didn't seem to make any difference to Hope—the famous and anonymous were comingled in this gallery of show biz friendships.

I even spotted a couple of pictures of Natty. He was younger then, but had the same sparkling eyes and narrow-mouth smile, especially as he had his arm draped over the broad shoulder of a younger Hope White wearing a chorus girl outfit. Her long legs and ample bosom were on professional display but her eyes were all her own. Cornflower blue, sparkling and smart.

My earlier opinion had been dead on: Hope White had been something then, and she was something now.

"Would you like a drink, dearie?" she asked.

"Do have any hemlock?"

She thought about it.

"No," she said, "but I have Haig&Haig."

Soothing as it might have been to sit in that hothouse and get pleasantly stewed, I still had a job to do: find Nathan Silverstein and get him back to Palm Desert.

"A Coke, please?"

"One Coke," she said brightly, "coming up!"

"How long have you known Nathan?!" I could hear her in the kitchen messing around with an ice cube tray.

"A long time!"

"Did you date him?"

"Honey, I *carbon*–dated him," Hope said as she came in with the Coke, which was in one of those old soda fountain glasses. She had a martini for herself.

She sat down on the couch next to me.

"I met him in the bad old days when he was doing the beach movies," she continued. "He hated them but was paying about three alimonies at the time so he needed the money. Mind you, he was no spring chicken even then. He used to say, 'I'd like to be a has-been, but I don't have the money.'"

"I think I saw a few minutes of one of those movies on TV one night," I said.

"You must have been up late," Hope said. "They were awful! And they gave poor Natty stupid lines to say. He hated them! The poor little honey was so unhappy, and he used to come to town to try and have a few laughs. I was still in the line in those days—I think it was at Harrah's—and Natty came backstage after the show and asked me out."

"Did you know who he was?"

She sipped her martini and smiled. "Oh sure. In this town you make it your business to know who's out front, so I knew Natty Silver was in the house. But I never thought I'd step out with him."

"Why did you?"

She seemed to give this question some serious thought, then she said, "He was just so funny."

She must have seen the quizzical look on my face, because she leaned forward, patted my hand, and said, "Let me tell you a secret, honey: You make a girl laugh and she'll make you smile, if you know what I mean."

And she blushed.

"Miss White, do you know where he is?"

"I don't know," she said. "Honest Injun, I left him at the Mirage."

"He checked out."

She opened her cornflower eyes nice and wide, smiled, shrugged, and finished her drink.

"Do you have an idea where he might have gone?" I asked.

"Honey," she said, "Natty Silver was once a headliner in this town. He can go anywhere he wants. This isn't New York or Hollywood. Las Vegas has a memory."

That's what I was banking on.

I thanked her and got up to leave.

"Do you have a girl, Neal?" she asked me at the door.

"A fiancée, actually."

"Do you make her laugh?"

"Oh, she thinks I'm a stitch."

I don't think she bought it, because she said, "Have Natty give you some good jokes."

If I can find him, Hope. If I can find him.

Chapter 4

I LEFT THE JEEP WITH THE VALET-PARKING GUYS and walked into the lobby of the Sands. I hung around the high-roller blackjack tables and made myself conspicuous until I saw a barrel-chested guy who gave me a twice-over.

I walked over to him.

"I'd like to see Mickey the C," I said.

"And you are?"

"Neal Carey."

"Does Mickey know you, Neal Carey?"

"No," I said. "But he knows people who know my boss."

"Give me names, Neal Carey."

"Joe Graham, Ed Levine, Ethan Kitteredge."

"Who do they know?"

"People in Providence," I said. "People in New York."

All kinds of people in both places. But in this case, "people" referred specifically to wise guys, mobbed-up guys, connected guys. See, Friends of the Family did all sorts of confidential things for its rich and influential clients, and if you're going to do confidential things for anybody in New York and Providence, you're bound to make some connections with the mob.

The same might be said of Las Vegas, which is what brought me to the Sands Hotel to talk with Mickey the C. I'd never met Mickey the C, but I'd heard about him since I was a kid.

The guy thought about it for a second and said, "Why don't you sit down and have a drink?"

"Thanks."

I found an empty barstool and ordered a beer. The bartender waved me off when I tried to pay for it

The Sands Hotel was a big contrast to the Nugget. It was sleek, stylish, and looked like serious money. It was run by serious people, too, which is why I had come here after Hope said she had no idea where Nathan had gone after their matinee romance.

I sipped my beer and watched the high-rollers, Armani-clad guys escorted by skinny blondes in black sheath dresses, win and lose at blackjack. Mickey the C was probably watching me on a monitor and making the necessary calls.

A few minutes later the barrel-chested guy came back and said, "Neal Carey, Mickey would like to see you."

I followed him upstairs to the security room, where somber men and women sat staring into monitors, watching the doors and the tables. The watchers could punch a few buttons and zoom in on a dealer's hands or a player's face or an individual coming through a door. The owners of serious casinos liked to know who came in and out of their places. They hired people like Mickey the C to know these things.

Mickey the C was in his early sixties but looked younger, which I attributed to a daily regimen of razor cuts, manicures, steam baths, and massages. Mickey was wearing a conservative gray suit that cost at least a thousand bucks, a monogrammed white shirt and an Italian print tie. His black Oxford shoes were polished to a high shine.

Mickey the C was serious people.

We shook hands.

"Neal," he said. "It's a late Sunday night on the East Coast so I didn't make the phone calls I probably should make, so I hope you're not screwing around."

"I'm on the job, Mr. C."

"I know who you are," Mickey said. "You're Joe Graham's gofer."

"Yes, sir."

Well, it was accurate enough.

"You did a big favor for some people in Providence a while ago," Mickey said.

"I was doing my job and it coincidentally worked out for them," I answered, ever modest.

"Anyway you're good people," Mickey said. "Why are you reaching out?"

"I messed up."

I told Mickey about Nathan Silverstein.

Mickey laughed and said, "Natty Silver gave you the slip?"

"That's what it comes down to."

Mickey the C chuckled, then said, "Why don't you have another beer and relax. I'll put a call out. Everyone in town knows Natty, we'll have him in maybe half an hour."

"That's why I came to you, Mr. C."

It wasn't just shameless brownnosing, it was also true.

Mickey said, "That's one smart thing you did today, anyway."

"I knew there was something."

"Take it easy, kid," Mickey said. "Nice to meet to you."

"Thanks for taking the time, sir."

"You have good manners," Mickey the C said. "Joe Graham did you okay."

Yeah, he did.

It took two beers instead of one, but I had just drained the second one when the barrel-chested guy found me at the bar and said, "Mr. Silver is at the Flamingo, in the Palm Room. Their guy is watching him till you get there."

I thanked him and left a tip for the bartender that was more than the beers would have been. Anything less would have been bad manners.

As I stepped down down into The Palm Room I heard Natty say, "Guy comes home and finds his wife rubbing her breasts with newspaper. He asks her what she's doing. She says, 'I read in a magazine that if you rub your breasts with newspaper they'll get bigger.' "

There was an expectant chuckle from the small crowd in the cocktail bar. (I was going to say a "titter of laughter," but I thought better of it.) Natty waited out the laugh, then continued, "The guy says, 'Newspaper? You should try toilet paper.' The wife says, 'Toilet paper? Why?' and the guy says, 'Well, it worked on your *ass*'."

The dozen or so people in the room roared. Didn't laugh—*roared*. I slipped into a booth at the back and hoped Natty didn't see me from the tiny stage. I looked around for the plainclothes security, made him in about three seconds, and nodded. The guy gave me a quick wave and strolled out.

It wasn't too tough to reconstruct what had been happening. The piano player, a young guy with slicked-back black hair, was sitting back on his bench, relaxing, sharing the fun, and figuring his tip jar wasn't going to suffer because the customers were getting some free laughs. The few drinkers in the place just looked surprised and delighted that this impromptu stand-up routine had started from this ancient guy they maybe recognized from TV.

And Natty Silver was having fun. Standing on that shitty little stage, leaning on his cane, eyes sparkling, teasing the crowd with his deadpan delivery and killer timing.

"Guy and a dog walk into a bar . . ." he was saying.

I checked my watch. If I grabbed Natty right now we could still make the plane and I could wrap up this errand. It would be a simple matter of getting up, easing Natty off the stage and grabbing a cab to the airport. Otherwise we'd miss the last flight to Palm Springs and that would mean spending the night in Vegas. Another night away from the old thesis, another night away from Karen.

It would mean an extra day of babysitting an old man who had a seemingly endless repertoire of old jokes.

I started to slide out of the booth.

Shit, I thought. Shit, shit shit.

I signaled the waitress, ordered a scotch rocks and sat back in the banquette.

What's another night? I thought. I had a lot of them and Natty Silver probably didn't.

"Guy says to the dog, 'You never behaved this way before . . .' "

Natty Silver looked very much alive as he teased the punch line.

"Dog says, 'I never had money before.' "

Hope was right: Natty Silver was very funny.

Chapter 5

"YOU WANT WHAT?" I ASKED NATTY AS WE LEFT
the Flamingo and headed back to the Mirage.

"Chocolate cake," he said.

"It's ten-thirty at night."

"What, chocolate cake disappears at ten?" he asked.
"There's a law, all chocolate cake has to become angel
food cake by ten-fifteen? We're run by chocolate-cake
Nazis now?"

I wasn't sure I even wanted to contemplate the image
of a chocolate-cake Nazi, so I just sighed. "Where can we
get chocolate cake?"

"You're the detective," Nate snapped. "Find some."

"I'm not a detective."

"No, you're an 'escort' with no bazookas."

I was about to say, given the cantilevered architecture
of Hope White's build, that he had more than filled his

bazooka quota for the day, but I decided he'd have a punch line for that and I didn't want to hear it.

I decided to take a professional approach.

"Look," I said. "Here's what we're going to do. We're going to go get your damn chocolate cake. Then we're going back to the Mirage and then we're going to bed. *Then* we're going to get up early and catch the first flight back to Palm Springs. No booze, no broads, no pastry. Got it?"

He looked at me with those little bird-eyes.

"No breakfast?"

It did sound a little harsh.

"We can have breakfast," I relented.

"What?"

"What 'what'?"

"What 'what what'?" he asked. "What's for breakfast?"

"I don't know," I moaned. "Bacon and eggs."

"Eggs?!" he snapped. "What, are you trying to kill me?"

I hadn't been, but the concept didn't entirely lack appeal at the moment.

But assuming it was a rhetorical question, I didn't answer.

"And bacon?" he asked indignantly.

"What's wrong with bacon?"

Apparently giving up on talking directly to me Nate mumbled to no one in particular, "He wants to feed bacon and eggs to an old Jew with a heart condition."

"I didn't know you had a heart condition," I said.

"I'm eighty-six years old," Nate answered. "That *is* a heart condition."

"Look, you can have gefilte fish and matzo balls for breakfast. I don't care."

"What about the chocolate cake?"

"For breakfast?"

"Now."

I knew that. I was just giving him back a little, you know.

"I have an idea," I said.

"Excuse me, but I'm skeptical."

"Why don't we go back to the Mirage and order the chocolate cake from room service?"

"What are you, crazy?" he asked. "Room-service prices?"

I didn't care. I had the company's gold card. With an American Express Gold Card in Vegas you could get a whole cake and someone to jump out of it if you wanted.

Anyway, that's what we did. (No, not the jumping-out part, just the cake part.) I could tell he was wearing out, so he didn't give me too much of a fight. And on a Sunday night it was no problem extending his room. So Nate sat in his underwear eating his cake and watching old movies on TV while I called Karen.

"Hi," I said. "What are you doing?"

"Knitting."

"The only thing I've ever seen you knit is your brow," I said.

Which was not overly bright on my part, but I was starting to get annoyed with the baby thing.

"You can be such a jerk," she said.

"I know."

"Don't think admitting it is going to get you off the hook," she said. "And I've been thinking."

Maybe, I hoped, she'd been thinking that getting pregnant right away was a tad premature and that we should wait until we've been married two or ten years. And that she was knitting me a sweater or a scarf or something.

"What have you been thinking?" I asked as gently as I could. You know, to let her ease into backing down.

"I've been thinking," she said, "that you're not okay with parenthood because you never knew your own father and your mother was a heroin-addicted prostitute who didn't nurture you and that you haven't really dealt with your suppressed rage sufficiently to surrender your own childhood and adopt adult responsibilities."

Oh.

"So you want me to come in every Tuesday, Doctor?" I asked.

"See, there's that hostility."

"Christ, I don't know why I'd be hostile!" I yelled.

"I think it's healthy that you're working out your anger," she said casually.

"I am not working out my goddamned anger!!!" I screeched.

"You don't have to get mad," she said.

And hung up.

Without taking his eyes off the television Nate said, "I went to a child psychiatrist once."

"Kid didn't do me any good at all," we said at the same time.

Nate looked at me with renewed respect.

Okay, not exactly respect. Call it affection.

All right, he looked at me with a near absence of total contempt, let's put it that way.

Nate looked at me with a renewed near absence of total contempt.

Then he fell asleep.

I took the plate and fork off his lap, lay his head back on his pillow and covered him with a sheet and blanket. Then I set the alarm and climbed into the other twin bed.

Nurturing, I thought. Suppressed rage. Surrender my childhood. Accept adult responsibilities.

We hadn't hadn't even had the kid yet and already I felt exhausted.

I told myself to forget about it and just go to sleep. Sleep would be good. Sleep would be great. All I had to do was lie there and not worry about suppressing or surrendering or accepting anything.

Just sleep.

Then Nathan started snoring.

I have heard snoring. This might be ungallant, but in the interest of honesty, Karen snores. Especially in the winter when she pulls the blankets completely over her head and makes a noise that is not so much a snore as it is a pre-suffocation death rattle. I wake up and open an air hole in the blankets for her and the snoring stops.

But I hadn't ever heard anything like Nathan's snoring. I had never heard a sound like that before in my life. It wasn't even a human sound, nor a sound that resembled any currently recognized species. No, it had a sort unnatural resonance to it, kind of like the bellows of hell opening and closing, or as if Bigfoot had somehow stolen into the body of an old man and fallen blissfully asleep.

As Nathan was.

He didn't have the blankets pulled up over his head, either. Although I thought about arranging it, and maybe forgetting about the airhole.

I didn't, though. I just lay there awake thinking about babies and stuff.

Chapter 6

AFTER A REFRESHING TWENTY MINUTES OF SLEEP
I got up, showered, and changed into yesterday's stale,
sweaty clothes. Then I woke up Nathan.

"You snore," he said. "I hardly slept a wink."

"Good morning," I said.

I ordered room service again for breakfast. I didn't
want to take a chance that Nate would meet some other
old love while gumming his oatmeal in the coffee shop.

The dirty rotten old bastard ordered two eggs over
easy, *bacon,* a cinnamon roll, a Bloody Mary, tea, and dry
toast.

"Dry toast?" I asked.

"Cholesterol," he mumbled while sucking down a strip
of bacon.

"I thought you were Jewish," I said, pointing my fork
at the surviving bacon.

"I am," Nate answered. "But not a fanatic. And order your own bacon."

He tried to stab me with his fork.

I chewed on my blueberry muffin and worked on the image of a nice airplane jetting us to the Palm Springs airport. A quick limo ride to Palm Desert and blessed freedom.

"So?" Nathan asked.

"So what?"

"So, aren't you going to make conversation?" he asked. "What, were you raised by apes? You just stuff your mouth and don't talk? You're an escort with no bazookas, the least you can do is make conversation."

"More bacon?"

"That's conversation?" Nathan asked, stuffing his mouth with more bacon.

Conversation . . . conversation. I'd never been very good at conversation. It usually required talking to people.

"Okay," I said, after a few moments of intense concentration. "So, where do you live?"

Nathan looked at me as if I were an idiot.

Go figure, huh.

Then he said, "You're supposed to take me home, you don't know where it is?"

"I know where it is," I said. "I meant, what's it like?"

"It's a townhouse," he said. "Although why they call it a townhouse I don't know because there's no town. It's in a resort complex right on the golf course."

"Oh, that's nice."

"Why is that nice?"

"So you can just pop out your door and play a nice round of golf," I said.

"I hate golf," Nathan said.

"Then why—"

"Because that's where they built the townhouse," he said. "Away from the town and on the golf course. What was I supposed to do?"

"Uhhhh, buy a different townhouse?"

"Away from the golf course?"

"Yeah . . ."

"Then I couldn't watch them."

"Watch who?"

"The golfers," Nathan said. He lit a cigarette.

My muffin was turning to sawdust in my mouth.

"But you hate golf," I said.

"More than I hate golf," Nathan said, "I hate golfers."

"So?"

"So the golfers who play golf outside my townhouse?"

"Yes?"

"They stink," he said. He took a long drag of the cigarette then spent the next thirty seconds coughing. "I love to watch them play because I hate them and they stink. I love to watch them get red in the face, say dirty words and bang their clubs into trees. This is fun for me, I'm eighty-six."

"I hate golf, too," I said. "In my opinion the only thing that could improve the game of golf is snipers."

I feel that this would really speed up the game. Instead of standing out there forever contemplating the three feet of grass between them and the cup, golfers in my version of the game would be *sprinting* onto the green, taking a running whack at the ball and diving for the sand trap as bullets stitched at their heels.

It would have a sartorial benefit as well: I mean, you could forget the bright pink shirts and the canary-yellow rayon slacks, right?

Nathan looked at me very seriously.

"Snipers," he said.

"Snipers."

"That's funny," he said. "You said a funny thing."

"Thank you."

"Who'd have thought?" Nathan asked. Then he blew a smoke ring in my face.

We finished breakfast, checked out, and took a taxi to the airport. I whipped out the old gold card, bought two tickets on the next flight and steered Nathan toward the concourse.

We sat at the gate for half an hour while he entertained me with jokes that were doubtless painted on the walls of the Lascaux caverns. After an eternity or two the flight attendant announced it was time to board.

Then Nathan said, "I'm afraid to fly."

"It's perfectly safe."

"What, you never heard of a plane crashing?"

"You stand more chance of dying in a car on the way to the airport than you do in the airplane," I said.

I'd heard this statistic from someone and it sounded right. Of course, I'd heard it in New York, where you were in more danger in even a *parked* car than you were in an airplane.

"It's not the dying I'm afraid of," he said.

"Then what is it?"

"It's the *crashing*."

"Now boarding," the stewardess said with that polite urgency they get when *you're* causing *them* delays.

"We're coming," I told her.

"Speak for yourself," Nate said. "If God had meant man to fly, He'd have given him—"

"Airplanes," I said. I'd describe myself as having said this through tightly clenched jaws except it might be misinterpreted as hostile.

"I'm not getting on that thing," Nate said.

"Final call," the stewardess warbled.

"We'll only be in the air for an hour," I said to Nate.

"Hopefully," he said.

"The great majority of crashes take place on takeoff or landing," I answered.

Which clinched it for Nate.

"I'm not getting on," he said.

"Yes you are."

"No."

"Yes."

"No."

"Yes!"

"Yes or no, gentlemen?" said the stewardess.

"What are you going to do?" Nate asked me. "Make me get on the plane?"

"If necessary," I said through tightly clenched jaws.

"Go ahead," Nate said. "Give me a beating."

Nate dug in, as much as an eighty-six-year-old man can be said to dig in. He stood wobbling on his feet, his cane unfirmly planted in the carpet, his watery blue eyes staring at me in defiance.

The old fart had me and he knew it. What *was* I going to do?

Nothing, that's what.

I mean, I could hardly grab an old man by the lapels and drag him kicking, screaming and kvetching onto the plane. And the stewardess was looking at me with one of those "I'm about to call security to come and pound you into a pulp" glares.

"I don't really beat him," I said to her. "He's joking."

"Some joke," she said. "Are you a relative of his?"

"No," I answered. "If I were related to him I wouldn't be standing here smiling through my teeth—I'd be sawing my own head off."

"What are you to this gentleman?" she asked in a voice that indicated that she was contemplating a 911 call.

"A friend," I said.

"Some friend," she said.

"He's my grandson," Nate said.

"God forbid."

"He's my grandson, the ungrateful little bastard," Nate said. "He wants I should die of fright on the airplane so he can inherit."

"That's ridiculous, I—"

"Well, you can forget it, because you're out of the will!" He turned to the stewardess. "You're my witness!"

The stewardess was down the jetway in a shot. After *snake-eyes,* the word *witness* might be the least popular word in Nevada.

Without removing his gaze from the stewardess's rear end Nate said, "See what you did?"

"Gee, I guess we'll drive," I said.

"Driving is better," Nate agreed.

Yeah right, I thought. Five hours there, two hours to get Nate settled, then another ten hours' drive back to Austin. Oh yeah, driving is much better.

As we were walking out to get a cab back to the Mirage to pick up the car, the thought finally occurred to me.

"Mr. Silverstein?" I asked.

"Yeeess?" he warbled in the stylized tone of a burlesque top banana.

"How did you get to Las Vegas?"

"I flew," he said.

Of course.

Then Nate said happily, "This guy with a wooden eye goes to a dance . . ."

The valet pulled up the Jeep and I gave him a five. He trotted around and opened the door for Nate.

Nate just stood there and stared at the Jeep.

"What?" I asked.

"An army truck?" he said.

"A Jeep."

"You want me to ride all the way to Palm Springs in an army truck?"

"Actually, I wanted you to fly all the way to Palm Springs in a civilian aircraft," I said. "But you wanted to drive."

"Not in an army truck."

"You're a Quaker now?"

"Bouncing," Nate said.

"Bouncing?"

"You think my kidneys are made of steel?!" he hollered. "My bladder is what, a rock? My back, my spine, my neck? You want from the bouncing they should snap?"

Yes.

"I'm not riding in that," he said.

"How about if we get a rope and I tow you behind?"

"Funny guy."

"Get in," I said.

"Forget it."

"Please."

"No."

"Just get in," I whined.

"No."

"I'll give you money."

"Money I got," Nate said. "But you can never replace your health."

So I tried one of things I'd seen parents do with four-year-olds. I got into the driver's seat, turned the key, and said, "Okay, I'm leaving."

"So go."

"I'm leaving now," I said in the same singsong tone I'd heard send the little rug-rats sprinting for Mommy and Daddy's departing heels.

"So leave already," Nate said.

I put the Jeep into drive and started to ease out of the parking circle. I could see Nate in the rearview mirror leaning on his cane, staring resolutely into space, his little knees wobbling.

"Good-bye!" I yelled.

He didn't answer.

> > >

After a pleasant hour in the rent-a-car line I was rewarded with the keys, unlimited mileage and a full tank of gas. I grabbed Nate from the lounge where he was . . . well, *lounging*, and dragged him out to the parking lot.

"So what kind of car did you get?" he asked.

"Blue."

We walked out to slot A-16, where was parked a lovely blue sedan with big cushioned seats.

"This is a Japanese car," Nate said.

"I guess so."

"What?" he snapped. "You never heard of Pearl Harbor?"

The nice girl behind the counter said, "Back already?"

I nodded.

"Don't you like the car?" she asked. "I can upgrade you to a BMW for only eighteen extra dollars a day."

"BMW," I mulled aloud. "That stands for Bavarian Motor Works, right?"

"You want it?"

"I don't think so."

"A Lexus?"

"No Japanese cars," I said. "No German cars."

"Huh?"

"I cannot rent any car made in the former Axis powers."

She looked on her computer screen.

"How about a nice Jeep?" she asked.

An hour later I walked Nate out to a Chevy Cavalier and said, "Sit in it."

"What did you think, I was going to stand?"

"No," I said. "Sit in it now."

He sat down.

"Do you like the seat?" I asked. "Are you comfortable?"

"It's nice."

"Made in Detroit," I said. "Any problems with its city of origin? No beef with the General Motors corporation? The color? It's red, you know. No hang-ups there? No unfortunate associations with the Bolsheviks?"

"Are we going to go, or what?"

"We're going to go," I said, and hustled into the driver's seat before he could change his mind. I turned the ignition and shifted into reverse.

"Go ahead," Nate said. "And back up."

Chapter 7

I LOVE THE DESERT.

The desert is not boring, as some would have you believe. Although I am, as are most private eyes, a connoisieur of boredom. Boredom is our business, as we spend most of our time waiting for other people to do interesting things (boring), or poring over paperwork (boring), or writing post-investigation reports (very boring). But I basically like boredom, because in this business if something boring isn't happening it usually means that something scary is. So boring is good.

So is the desert, even though it's not boring.

Normally a long desert drive is a thing of joy and beauty to me. I love the colors—the muted, subtle shades of tans, browns, and lavenders. I revel in the enormous expanse of open blue sky. I worship the sheer, vast emptiness, the solitude, the quiet.

But after one hour on this particular drive on Interstate 15 through the Nevada desert I was ready to reach down my throat with a pair of pliers and pull my own lungs out. If I'd had a gun I would have shot myself so I wouldn't have to live with the memory of an hour trapped in a car with Nathan Silverstein, aka Natty Silver.

It started about five minutes into the drive when he said, "Ask me who's on first."

"No thanks."

"Ask me who's on first!"

"No."

He started to pout.

Now, I know about pouting. Not for nothing has Karen been known to refer to me as The Incredible Sulk. I am a marathon pouter, a deep Celtic brooder of the darkest sort. But I was a piker compared to Natty Silver. Natty Silver's unhappiness hung in the confined air of the car like a thick gray cloud. No—not a cloud, something more solid. It filled the car like some sort of toxic Jell-O that hardened around my feet then jiggled up to my neck until I was choking in misery.

Natty could pout.

I broke.

"Who's on first?" I asked, hating myself for the craven, belly-up dog that I was.

"Right," he answered happily.

"Right's on first?"

"No, who's on first," he said triumphantly.

I chuckled appreciatively and stopped.

He said, "So what's the matter?"

"Nothing's the matter."

"So?"

"So nothing."

"What, you don't know the bit?"

"I know the bit," I said. "It's an old Abbott and Costello routine."

"Abbott and Costello didn't invent that sketch," Nathan said contemptuously. "Phil Gold and I were doing 'Who's on First' when Lou Costello was shitting his diapers!"

"Okay."

"I taught Lou Costello 'Who's on First'!"

"When he was in diapers?" I asked.

"When he was so wet behind the ears he needed a towel," Natty said. "It was at Minsky's. Minsky's, now *there* was a burlesque house. Those Minskys knew burlesque. They knew naughty from dirty. Until the Decency League shut them down Minsky's was the cleanest burlesque house in the world. A classy place, and the girls were not hookers. But speaking of hookers, you heard the one about the hooker who says to eighty-six-year-old Mr. Birnbaum, 'I'm here to give you super sex.' Birnbaum says, 'I'll take the soup.' "

I was doing about seventy. If I opened my door and rolled out now, how badly could it hurt?

"Now, Arthur Minsky loved good pastrami," Nathan said, "and he knew deli. You could not put inferior delicatessen in front of Arthur Minsky, who by the way, was a gentleman. A refined man. Arthur Minsky would not allow filth in his theaters and he knew the difference between naughty and dirty. I remember one time Eileen the Irish Dream wanted to respond to an unkind review which intimated that she was not a natural redhead, with a visual display that she was, and Arthur put his foot down.

"Of course, Eileen was a nasty piece of work. A tramp. Kept company with a no-goodnik mobster from the Schultz gang named Benny the Blade. Wore spats. Trash.

"So one day Arthur sends out the new kid, an Irish kid. Stupid like you. Arthur sends the kid to Wolff's to get him a pastrami on rye with Russian mustard. Wolff's had great pastrami, wonderful pastrami. Wolff knew delicatessen. In those days you could go to a deli and get a sandwich would choke a horse for twenty-five cents and it was good deli. Not this trash they serve you today. They just opened a deli in Palm Desert. Two Jews from Los Angeles open a deli and charge seven bucks for a sandwich which is trash. Stringy fat. It got caught between my teeth, right here. I was with Murray Koppelman. Do you know Murray? Had a for-shit comedy show on CBS? 'Murray, Murray, Murray' they used to sing? Murray would come out surrounded by shiksas with legs to their chins and roll his eyes. Audience would scream, I don't know why. I *do* know why, free tickets, that's why, and some boob holding up a card says *Laugh.* We didn't have these cards in burlesque. Our audience was waiting to see girls take off their clothes. We had to be funny. If you held up a card that says *Laugh* in a burlesque house, they would throw garbage at you and they would be right.

"I saw that happen one afternoon to a magician. The Great Bandolini. Magicians always had to give themselves Italian names, I don't know why. You never saw a magician named 'The Great Lefkowitz.' Anyway, Bandolini had an act where he would pull doves from his coat. You've seen the act. First he opens his coat, no doves. He says some words in Italian, opens the coat again, and *bingo*—doves. Except, this one afternoon he is coming in from Philadelphia on the train and the porters lose the case that has Bandolini's doves in it. What's Bandolini going to do? He goes to talk to Myra DeLovely who had a striptease act called Myra DeLovely and her Doves of Love, in which Myra stripped and the doves landed in strategic spots to prevent the Decency League from shutting her down. Bandolini asks can he borrow the doves to make them appear out of his coat. Myra is reluctant, but a good sport, and she says okay.

"What nobody thinks about is that these doves are not trained to sit quietly hiding in the secret pockets of the coat. Bandolini gets onstage, opens the coat, and says, 'No doves'—except that there *are* doves. There are doves rustling around, cooing, flapping their wings. The audience boos, the doves get spooked and fly into the house. The doves are flying around the ceiling, very upset, and you know what a nervous dove does. So now you've got Bandolini yelling, the audience booing, and the doves are shitting all over them. Myra comes out screaming at Bandolini, hitting him. Audience starts throwing garbage. Tomatoes, hard-boiled eggs, even liverwurst they threw. Bonbons they threw.

"Myra slips on a bonbon, throws her hip out of joint. A very bad injury for a burlesque girl. Nowadays she'd sue, of course, but people didn't sue in those days. Myra goes to a doctor in Gramercy Park, Dr. LaFramboise, a Frenchman. This LaFramboise puts her hip back into joint and his own joint . . . You get the idea. Myra gets in a family way and the doctor acts like a mensch and marries her. They have a daughter who grows up to be a singer, except this girl cannot carry a tune in a bucket. The girl cannot sing! Myra and LaFramboise don't know what to do! What to do with a daughter who is a singer who can't sing?! Fortunately she marries the son of LaFramboise's accountant, a kid named Koppelman. Koppelman and this girl who can't sing produce a son who can't get a laugh except when they hold up a card that says *Laugh* and that turns out to be the for-shit comic, my good friend Murray Koppelman. 'Murray, Murray, Murray.'

"So Murray says, 'Nate, you have a string of fat stuck between your teeth.' I think it's one of Murray's stupid jokes, because without his writers, let's face it, Murray Koppelman is not funny. So I say, 'Murray, what? This is funny? Food-in-your-teeth jokes?' He says he's serious, so I turn to this lady at the next table and ask, 'Do I have a string of fat stuck between my teeth?' and she says, 'Yes, you do. You do have a string of fat stuck between your teeth, right here,' and she shows me on her teeth!

64

"The woman had a beautiful mouth. I said, 'Do you go to Dr. Kaufman?' She says, 'No, I go to Dr. Millman.'

" 'Millman?' I say. 'Millman is a crook!' She says, 'Millman is my nephew!' I say, 'Sol Millman?' She says, 'No, *Sam* Millman.' And I say, 'That's good. I was thinking of Sol Millman who is the crook'—so I covered myself there. But that Sam Millman is a crook who will take the gold right out of your mouth. Now Kaufman, there's a dentist.

"Kaufman is the dentist who fixes my teeth after I crack one with a fork trying to get the string of fat out which is what comes from cheap pastrami. Now at Wolff's they would never give you stringy, fatty pastrami. Wolff knew delicatessen. He knew good delicatessen from *drech*. Arthur Minsky always sent out to Wolff's. Nothing else would do for Arthur Minsky who was a man of refinement. A gentleman, Arthur Minsky.

"So the Irish kid comes back with the sandwich and puts the bag on Arthur's desk. Arthur is in the middle of telling Eileen the Irish Dream that never again will she remove her g-string on the runway of Minsky's no matter what any critic writes and Benny the Blade starts yelling that Eileen has to redeem her honor because she has been slandered and Arthur says that any man who wears spats should perhaps not open his mouth on matters concerning taste.

"They are having this discussion when the Irish kid who was stupid like you sets the sandwich down on Arthur's desk, and Arthur is arguing with Benny as he bites into the sandwich and he's saying, 'Benny, excuse me, I don't tell you how to run numbers, please do not tell me how to run—This is salami!!'

"Arthur can't believe it, Eileen can't believe it, Benny can't believe it, even I can't believe it because I am sitting there waiting to talk to Arthur about what we're going to do with Phil Gold, who is out again on a bender, and who am I supposed to do 'Who's on First' with?

"Arthur starts to laugh, Eileen starts to laugh, Benny the Blade starts to laugh and then I start to laugh and this Irish kid says, 'What?' and Arthur says, 'This is the last time I send a goy to get deli.' He tousles the kid's hair and tells him, 'I said pastrami, not salami.' This kid didn't know the difference between—"

"DON'T YOU EVER SHUT UP?!"

Okay. I'm not proud of it. But that's what I yelled. No excuses. I just lost it.

I know, I know. How could I be so mean to a sweet old man like Nathan Silverstein who was merely indulging in some old memories to kill a little time on a long car trip? All I can say in my own defense is that you weren't in the car with him.

Well, he shut up, all right. After I screamed, he turned those watery little eyes to me, looked very hurt, then slowly turned face forward and maintained a total, dignified silence. ✦

Which was worse than the monologue.

Not at first. At first it was wonderful, sweet silence. Blessed solitude with a slight underlay of guilt, but I was willing to live with that.

At first. Then it grew heavier. And heavier. As the miles between Nevada and California peeled away the weight of the guilt pressed down on my shoulders like two anvils. How could I be so mean to a sweet old man like Nathan Silverstein who was merely indulging in some old memories to kill a little time on a long car trip?

So after half an hour of total silence I asked, "Who's on first?'

Silence.

"Who's on first?" I repeated.

He just stared straight ahead.

"Please," I wheedled. "Please," I whined.

But after almost twenty-four hours of almost unceasing irritation I finally got my wish: Nathan Silverstein wouldn't talk to me.

After about one hour of silence torture later I pulled over into one of those gas station–cum–junk food places.

"Do you have to use the bathroom?" I asked.

No answer.

"Do you?" I repeated.

Same response.

"Well, I do," I said. "So I tell you what: I'll go in and use the bathroom, then I'll come back out and if you want to go in, you can. How's that?"

Nathan just stared ahead. For a second I thought he was dead except that I could see his frail little chest breathing.

"Okay, here I go," I said.

I went in and stood at the urinal wondering if and

when Nathan was ever going to forgive me. I really did feel awful. I felt like hell.

Until I came back out and saw Nathan driving away.

The rotten old bastard had taken the car.

Chapter 8

THE STATE TROOPER WAS NOT AMUSED.

"Was the vehicle locked?" asked Trooper Darius.

We were standing in the gas-station parking lot where the temperature was only about 109.

"No," I said. "The car was not locked."

Even through his reflective sunglasses I could see the disdainful stare. Yeah, all right, I could imagine it, anyway.

"May I see the keys?" he asked.

"I don't have the keys."

A long, disgusted pause.

"You left the keys in the vehicle," he said.

"I left the keys in the vehicle."

"Your insurance company isn't going to like that."

"It's a rented car."

"Then your insurance company really isn't going to

like that," he said. "Have you reported the loss to the rental-car agency?"

"Not yet."

"You should."

"I will."

"License-plate number?"

"I don't know."

"Because it's a rental car."

"That's right."

"The rental agreement will have it," Trooper Darius said. "Don't tell me, it's in the vehicle."

"With the keys," I said.

He sighed a long-suffering sigh, then asked, "What kind of car is it?"

I thought about it for a few seconds.

"Red," I answered.

His hand twitched in unconscious yearning around his nightstick.

"What *make*?" he clarified.

Now I sighed.

"I know it's not Japanese or German," I said. This time he took the glasses off to stare at me. More of a squint, really, in the sun.

"I don't suppose it's much use asking you the year, right?" he said.

"I don't know a lot about cars," I said.

"No fooling."

"I'm from New York," I explained.

"Don't they have cars in New York?"

"Subway cars," I joked.

I should have had one of those cards that said *Laugh*.

"You want us to look for a red car," Trooper Darius said.

"I can identify the driver."

"How?" he asked.

"Because he was in the car."

"When?"

"When I was driving it," I said. "Before he took it."

Another long pause while the sun beat down on his Smokey the Bear hat and my bare, sweating head.

"The passenger stole the vehicle?" he asked.

"I'm not sure I'd say 'stole,' " I answered. "But, yes, the passenger took the car."

"You know the suspect."

"I'm afraid I do."

"Describe him."

"An older gentleman . . ." I began.

"How old?"

"Eighty-six."

I had never before seen a state trooper struggling not to laugh.

"An eighty-six-year-old man stole your car," he said.

"Well again, I wouldn't necessarily say—"

"Did he beat you up?" he asked.

"No, I—"

"Threaten you in any way?"

"No, you see—"

"Was he armed?"

"No," I said. "I went to use the bathroom and when I came out I saw him driving away. I thought he would turn around and come back, but—"

"Didn't the old man need to use the bathroom?" he asked. "Because usually—"

"That's what I thought, but he said he didn't."

"Now we know why."

"I guess so."

"Name?"

"Neal Carey."

"*His* name."

"I thought you meant my name."

"No, his name," said Trooper Darius. "I already know your name. Your name is Neal Carey."

"Right."

"Right."

We stood for a few seconds enjoying the sunshine.

"So what is it?" the trooper asked.

"What's what?"

"What's his name?" the trooper asked. "Take it slow, now. *His* name, not yours."

"Nathan Silverstein," I said. "Or Natty Silver."

"Which?"

"Both."

"How *many* eighty-six-year-old men stole your car?" he asked.

"Just one," I said.

"So we're on the lookout for a red car driven by an

eighty-six-year-old man named Nathaniel Silverstein aka Natty Silver," the trooper said.

"That about sums it up."

"Which way was he headed?"

"He went thataway," I said, pointing west.

"He could be a long way thataway," said the trooper.

"I don't think so."

"Why don't you think so?"

"Because he was driving about twenty miles an hour."

Trooper Darius thought for what seemed like a long time. Then he said, "Get in the car."

"The car's gone."

"*My* car."

"Oh."

We were cruising west on Interstate 15 when the trooper said, "I thought if we can catch up to the old man, and if everything checks out, then you can just get back in the driver's seat and you won't have to call the rental-car people or your insurance company and I won't have to file a stolen-vehicle report."

"I really appreciate that," I said. "Thank you."

We were doing eighty miles an hour so it wasn't long before we found the car in a ditch at the side of the road. We pulled over and I jumped out of the cruiser, my heart pounding. I was scared to death I'd find Natty slumped over the wheel, hurt or worse.

I jumped into the ditch and looked into the car.

Nathan wasn't in it.

Chapter 9

GRAHAM ANSWERED THE PHONE.

I'd been hoping he wasn't home so that I could leave a brief message after the beep. Something like, *"Hi, it's Neal. I'll call back."*

But Graham was home, watching an exhibition game between the New Orleans Saints and the San Diego Chargers.

And they call *me* mentally ill.

"Hi, Dad," I said.

"How's Palm Springs?" he asked. After a couple of seconds he added, "You lost him again, didn't you?"

"Yes."

"How do you keep misplacing an entire person?" Graham asked. "I can understand a watch, a wallet, a glove. But an entire human being?! Twice, in the space of less than twenty-four hours?! Who is this guy, Harry Houdini?"

Sort of. Because he had simply disappeared. When Trooper Darius and I got to the car, there was no sign at all of Nathan. He was just gone. Without a trace. We even looked for blood on the steering wheel and windshield, thinking that maybe he'd hit his head. There was none, thank God.

Nathan was just gone.

"What do you mean, 'blood on the dashboard'?" Graham asked. "I thought you were supposed to fly back."

"I thought so, too."

I told him about the scene at the airport. I told him about the Jeep and bouncing. I told him about Japanese cars, German cars—

"So what kind of car did you get?" he asked.

"Red, all right?!!" I hollered.

"Just asking."

I told him about "Who's on First," about Lou Costello, Arthur Minsky, pastrami, Murray Koppelman, Irene the Irish Dream, Myra and her Doves of Love . . .

Graham asked, "How did she train the doves to land . . . ?"

"I don't know!"

. . . about Benny the Blade, salami instead of pastrami, how I screamed at Nathan—

"That was hostile," Graham said.

I stopped. "Since when did you start using words like 'hostile'?"

"Since I talked to Karen earlier," he said.

"You talked to Karen?"

"I called to ask her if she's registered for her patterns," Graham said. "And she told me you were hostile."

"I'm starting to *get* hostile . . ."

"See?"

I swallowed hard and told him about pulling over at the gas station, about going into the men's room, about—

"You left the keys in the car and he took it," Graham said. "But you found the car again."

I told him about Trooper Darius.

"That's where the 'blood on the dashboard' thing comes in," Graham said.

"There wasn't any."

"Which is good," Graham said.

"Graham, I'm scared out of my wits. We checked at the trooper station, the Sheriff's Office. I called the hospitals, the morgue. What if—"

"Neal," Graham said, "somebody else probably saw him standing by the road and picked him up. Silverstein's probably halfway home by now."

"You think?"

"Sure," Graham said. "Listen, leave the cops my number. Then you drive to Palm Desert. Check the rest stops as you go, in case someone dropped him off and he's trying to call. Check in with me every two hours."

"Okay."

"You'll probably get to his house and find him in his living room watching *Wheel of Fortune*."

I started to feel better. Silverstein *was* probably sitting at home watching *Wheel of Fortune.* He was fine. Bored, but fine.

Thank God.

"Unless—" Graham said.

" *'Unless'?*"

"Unless," Graham said, "there's a reason Silverstein doesn't want to go home. . . ."

A reason?

Not wanting to go home?

What would make Graham think that Nathan doesn't want to go home? Just because he disappeared yesterday, wouldn't get on the airplane, wouldn't get in the Jeep, wouldn't get in a Toyota, a Mazda, a Nissan, a BMW or a Mercedes, then took the car, drove off, dumped the car and disappeared . . .

"You think he was stalling?" I asked.

"Maybe."

"Why wouldn't he want to go home?" I asked.

>)))

I asked Karen this question when I called her up.

"Before you say anything about sperm or hostility or knitting or anything," I said when she answered, "I need to talk to you."

"I'm listening."

I told her the entire odyssey (so far) of my experience with Nathan and finished with the question, "Why wouldn't Nathan want to go home?"

"Let me see," Karen said. "In Las Vegas he has booze, a girlfriend, and an audience. And chocolate cake. In Palm Desert he has . . . television, I guess. The more interesting question is, why would he want to go *home?*"

"I hadn't thought about it that way."

"Neal, he's a lonely old man who had some fun and company in Las Vegas," she said. "Then you hurt his pride so he decided he'd show you. And he did."

Yes, he did.

She said, "So go find him, apologize, and then talk to him about getting a nice condo in Las Vegas."

"Karen, my job is to get him home, not take care of him forever."

"Neal, life puts things in your way for a reason."

"You think so?"

"I know so."

This is a big difference between Karen and me. She thinks that life is a fated journey of challenges and discoveries. I think it's a random sequence of arbitrary occurrences. I also thought that she was veering dangerously close to the baby thing. If Karen decided that having a child right now was fate, I was doomed.

"I'm glad you're not mad at me anymore," I said.

"I didn't say that I wasn't mad at you," she said. "You said that you needed to talk. Now, when I tell you that I need to talk, which is about once a week, you listen, right? So when you tell me that you need to talk, which is once about every eight months or so, I'm going to listen because I love you. But I'm still royally pissed at you."

"*Royally* pissed?"

"Royally."

"Jesus."

"Damn straight."

She broke the silence by saying, "So go find Nathan Silverstein, get him settled, then come home and knock me up."

Click. Dial tone.

First things first, I thought. First find Nathan, then get him home.

Sigh. Then find out if he'd really rather live in Las Vegas. It shouldn't be too hard to convince Friends to get him organized with a nice little condo in Vegas. Maybe somewhere near the Great Hope White, so they could do whatever it was they did together. Then Nathan could happily totter around, smoke cigarettes, drink vodka, ogle women, eat chocolate cake, and perform impromptu stand-up routines in cocktail bars. Karen and Graham were right. What was I so worried about?

Where to begin, where to begin . . .

Chapter 10

THERE'S A LOT OF TALK THESE DAYS ABOUT THE learning curve. You know, you're "ahead of the curve," you're "behind the curve," etcetera. Well, on the issue of why Nathan didn't want to go back to his condo in Palm Desert, I wasn't ahead of the curve or behind the curve.

I was standing flat-footed and stupid *on* the curve and the car was speeding *around* the curve right at me.

In my defense, I didn't know then what I know now. At the time, I headed west through the desert on I-15 looking for the Nathan I knew nothing about. . . .

Listen, it ticked me off when I found out about it. I mean, when I finally had a chance to look at the following documents I thought something along the order of, *"Sure, now. Why didn't you show me this when it could have done me some good?"*

I don't want you thinking the same thing, so:

> > >

Craig D. Schaeffer
Attorney-at-Law
3615 Monterey
Palm Desert, CA

Ms. Pamela A. Holmstrum
Claims Superintendent
Western States Insurance Co.
801 Flower Street
Los Angeles, CA

17 July 1983

Dear Ms. Holmstrum,

Pursuant to your request that I evaluate the coverage situation *vis-à-vis* the fire that occurred to your insured, Mr. Heinz Muller, on 30 May, I undertook the following activities: I reviewed the fire inspector's reports and spoke with Captain MacKenzie of the Coachella Valley Consolidated Fire Department; I took recorded statements of Mr. Muller and his tenant, Mr. Abdullah; I reviewed various financial records of both Mr. Muller and Mr. Abdullah; I attempted to contact potential witnesses to the fire; and I reviewed the applicable statutory and case law relevant to the insurance coverage issues. (Please refer to Appendix A for a discussion of the applicable case law.)

Based on this preliminary investigation I offer the following thoughts:

It seems clear that the fire which destroyed the insured's house at 1385 Hopalong Way, Palm Desert, California, was incendiary in nature—that is, an arson fire. Sheriff's investigators found trace elements of incendiary material—to wit, gasoline—in the flooring and subflooring. Additionally, traces of wicks—in this case bed sheets twisted and laid out in various strings throughout the house—were also found. Also, sheriff's investigators state that this was a "hot" fire, a comment which might seem a redundancy on the surface, but which is actually a piece of jargon that refers to the relative temperature of the combustion, a "hot" fire being indicative of arson.

In English, Ms. Holmstrum, your insured's house went up like a torch.

Equally suspicious is the fact that your insured's tenant, Mr. Sami Abdullah (also your insured, as he has a rental policy with Western States Insurance Company), was out of town on a long weekend when the fire occurred. Mr. Abdullah states that he was in Las Vegas, but cannot remember the "precise name" of the hotel in which he stayed.

Mr. Muller, who resides in nearby Rancho Mirage, also seems to have been away that whole weekend. Mr. Muller states that he was in Big Bear, and offered hotel and restaurant receipts to validate this assertion.

As to Mr. Muller's claim for policy limits benefits under his homeowner's insurance policy, while we should by all means continue to investigate, I am afraid that, in the absence of any proof of Muller's involvement in the fire, you will owe such benefits. While it is true that Mr. Muller has been trying to sell the house at 1385 Hopalong Way, it does not appear that he has any apparent financial difficulties that would be a motive for arson. In fact, Mr. Muller seems, as much as we can determine from his complex financial records, to be doing rather well in the international import/export market. Furthermore, he seems to have an airtight alibi for the time of the fire.

As to Mr. Abdullah's claim for his personal property destroyed in the fire, I can only say that I have some personal doubts as to the legitimacy of Mr. Abdullah's claim that he had (as a partial sample): 28 Armani suits, 37 pairs of Gucci loafers, 52 silk shirts, 2 large-screen Sony television sets, a valuable 1965 Mustang in the garage and an Edward Hooper (sic) painting valued at $137,000. The claim becomes all the more preposterous when you consider that Mr. Abdullah can show no proof of employment for the past five years although he claims to have been making between "thirty to two hundred fifty thousand dollars" a year during that period as a "consultant."

I think you are well within your rights to deny Mr. Abdullah's claim, cancel his policy and sever his additional living-expense payments immediately, based on fraud and misrepresentation. Unfortunately, I do not believe that we have developed sufficient proof to deny Mr. Muller's claim, and advise that you pay him $600,000 forthwith.

If you have any questions, or if I may be of any further assistance, please do not hesitate to contact me.

Sincerely,
Craig Schaeffer, Esquire

> > >

Ms. Pamela A. Holmstrum
Claims Superintendent
Western States Insurance Co.
801 Flower Street
Los Angeles, CA

Craig D. Schaeffer
Attorney-at-Law
3615 Monterey
Palm Desert, CA

21 July 1983

Dear Mr. Schaeffer,

Thank you for your letter of the 17th inst. and for
your valuable coverage analysis. I have only one
question:

What are you, nuts?!

You know, I know—and if Helen Keller were
alive, she'd know—that Heinz Muller and Sami
Abdullah burned down this house. For God's sake,
Schaeffer, Muller had a $500,000 balloon payment
coming up. The damn house had been on the
market for fourteen months! It was either lose the
house or sell it to his insurance company. As to that
moke Sami Abdullah, you're damned right we're
canceling his policy. (By the way, have you asked to
see the little bastard's green card? Let him go back
to Beirut and file a phony claim there, see what
happens. Don't they cut off their hands or
something?)

Here's the deal, Craig: I'll pay Heinz Muller
policy limits on the same day a trained monkey

crawls out my butt singing "Tie A Yellow Ribbon
'Round the Old Oak Tree" in Polish.

Where are your balls, Craig? I didn't hire you to
roll over like a beaten dog.

Sincerely,
Pamela Holmstrum
Claims Superintendent
Western States Insurance Co.

> > >

Craig D. Schaeffer
Attorney-at-Law
3615 Monterey
Palm Desert, CA

Ms. Pamela A. Holmstrum
Claims Superintendent
Western States Insurance Co.
801 Flower Street
Los Angeles, CA

24 July 1983

Dear Ms. Holmstrum,

Thank you for your letter of the 21th inst. and
may I observe what a wonderful thing it is that the
attorney-client privilege allows us to have such a
frank and open exchange of views.

While I understand your reluctance to reward a
criminal act such as arson with a policy limits
payment, I would be remiss in my duty as your
attorney not to advise you to nevertheless do just
that.

You have no proof. You have no witnesses. If you deny this claim, Mr. Muller will most likely file a bad-faith lawsuit which could expose your company to a multimillion-dollar punitive-damages award.

Pamela, I know that you are new to this job and eager to impress your bosses and that at your tender age you nevertheless deserved this promotion. I am further sensitive to the fact that, as a young woman executive, you feel more than the usual pressure to show "toughness." I understand these things. Nevertheless—and again—my best opinion is to pay the $600,000 now or risk having a very large, multilingual, singing simian indeed force its egress from your digestive system, the hard way.

> Sincerely,
> Craig Schaeffer, Esquire

〉　〉　〉

By Fax

July 26, 1983

Dear Craig,

Too late. I denied both claims.

> Pamela

〉　〉　〉

By Fax

July 26, 1983

Dear Pamela,

He'll sue.

> Craig

> > >

By Fax

July 26, 1983

Dear Craig,

He doesn't have the *cajones.*

Pam

> > >

The Law Offices of Eugene E. Petkovitch
1500 Mitch Miller Boulevard
Palm Springs, CA

Ms. Pamela Holmstrum
Western States Insurance Co.
801 Flower Street
Los Angeles, CA

27 July 1983

Dear Ms. Holmstrum,

This letter is to put you on notice that I have filed
a lawsuit on behalf of my client and your insured, <u>Mr.
Heinz Muller</u>, for breach of contract and bad faith.
The conduct of both your claims department and
its coverage counsel, Attorney Craig Schaeffer,
has been despicable in the extreme. Your fraudulent,
oppressive and malicious attempts to violate the rights
of my client and avoid paying the insurance benefits
to which he is rightly entitled are flagrant violations
of both California law and common decency.

I am personally and professionally outraged—
OUTRAGED—that an insurance carrier in this day

and age would single out for oppressive treatment an individual just because that person happens to be a foreign immigrant. Immigration built this land, Ms. Holmstrum, lest you or Western States Insurance Company ever forget it!

Your conduct has been despicable!

I am certain that a California jury will send a message to the insurance industry—via a large punitive damages award—that this type of conduct will no longer be tolerated.

There is still time for you to avoid litigation.

My client, Mr. Heinz Muller, is generously willing to accept full policy benefits plus an additional $10,000,000 for the pain, suffering and humiliation that your Gestapo-like inquisition and jackboot investigative tactics have inflicted upon him. This sum represents far less than an outraged jury would award and saves you the cost of a long, expensive, and ultimately futile defense.

This offers expires at close of business, five working days hence, and will not be compromised or renewed.

Sincerely yours,
Eugene Petkovitch, Esquire

)))

The Law Offices of Eugene E. Petkovitch
1500 Mitch Miller Boulevard
Palm Springs, CA

Ms. Pamela Holmstrum
Western States Insurance Co.
801 Flower Street
Los Angeles, CA

27 July 1983

Dear Ms. Holmstrum,

This letter is to put you on notice that I have filed a lawsuit on behalf of my client and your insured, Mr. Amin "Sami" Abdullah, for breach of contract and bad faith. The conduct of both your claims department and its coverage counsel, Attorney Craig Schaeffer, has been despicable in the extreme. Your fraudulent, oppressive and malicious attempts to violate the rights of my client and avoid paying the insurance benefits to which he is rightly entitled are flagrant violations of both California law and common decency.

I am personally and professionally outraged— OUTRAGED—that an insurance carrier in this day and age would single out for oppressive treatment an individual just because that person happens to be a foreign immigrant. Immigration built this land, Ms. Holmstrum, lest you or Western States Insurance Company ever forget it!

Your conduct has been despicable!

I am certain that a California jury will send a message to the insurance industry—via a large punitive damages award—that this type of conduct will no longer be tolerated.

There is still time for you to avoid litigation.

My client, Mr. Amin 'Sami' Abdullah, is generously willing to accept full policy benefits plus an additional $5,000,000 for the pain, suffering and humiliation that your Gestapo-like inquisition and jackboot investigative tactics have inflicted upon him. This sum represents far less than an outraged jury would award, and saves you the cost of a long, expensive, and ultimately futile defense.

This offers expires at close of business, five
working days hence, and will not be compromised
or renewed.

> Sincerely yours,
> Eugene Petkovitch, Esquire

> ❯ ❯ ❯

> Ms. Pamela A. Holmstrum
> Claims Superintendent
> Western States Insurance Co.
> 801 Flower Street
> Los Angeles, CA

Craig D. Schaeffer
Attorney-at-Law
3615 Monterey
Palm Desert, CA

27 July 1983

Dear Craig,
    Please see attached correspondence from
Attorney Eugene Petkovitch on behalf of his clients,
our policyholders, Heinz Muller and Amin "Sami"
Abdullah.
    FIFTEEN MILLION DOLLARS!!!???
    *He sends us form letters demanding fifteen million
dollars?!*
    Who does this guy think he is?!

> Pam

> > >

Craig D. Schaeffer
Attorney-at-Law
3615 Monterey
Palm Desert, CA

Ms. Pamela A. Holmstrum
Claims Superintendent
Western States Insurance Co.
801 Flower Street
Los Angeles, CA

29 July 1983

Dear Pam,

You've never heard of Eugene "The Wolverine" Petkovitch?! Where have you been?

Eugene Petkovitch is the most despised, loathed, feared and respected plaintiff attorney in California, if not the known litigious world. Over the past ten years the Wolverine has hit every major insurance carrier in the state for seven- and eight-figure punitive damages awards.

When that security guard in mid-Wilshire shot the big toe off the would-be bank robber and the bank robber got $2,000,000? Eugene "The Wolverine" Petkovitch.

When the security guard sued the company that made the gunsight and won $3,000,000? Eugene Petkovitch.

When the would-be bank robber sued his insurance company for failing to pay his legal costs, citing "Chronic Recidivist Syndrome" and won $5,000,000? Eugene Petkovitch.

When the security guard sued his insurance company, the bank's insurance company, and the would-be robber's insurance company, citing "Severe Post-Victimization Stress Disorder" and won $6,000,000? Eugene Petkovitch.

These are just a few of the judicial highlights of the Wolverine's recent career.

The guy's cross-examinations are brutal. I've seen them. I remember. I wish I could forget.

I've seen hardened insurance executives break down and sob on the stand during one of Gene's cross-exams. I've seen homicide cops blubber like babies. I've seen guys develop permanent eye twitches and stutters. In fact, one of Gene's victims was a claims superintendent who happened to be a deaf mute. Gene crossed him *in sign language* and I swear the guy's hands were shaking. The jury concluded he was lying.

Eugene Petkovitch is Satan.

He rarely even has to go to trial anymore, everyone is that afraid of him. He just writes the demand letter, fills in the amount, and the insurance companies pay.

Pay the money, Pam. I'm begging you.

You don't want this trouble. I don't want this trouble.

> Sincerely,
> Craig

>))

Ms. Pamela A. Holmstrum
Claims Superintendent
Western States Insurance Co.
801 Flower Street
Los Angeles, CA

Craig D. Schaeffer
Attorney-at-Law
3615 Monterey
Palm Desert, CA

1 August 1983

Dear Craig,

Where have I been?

I've been in Nebraska, Craig, where—naive and old-fashioned as this may seem—we still take a dim view of extortion. I'll admit that I'm just the new kid here in sophisticated California—a hayseed, a hick, a corn-fed farm girl with the mud barely dry on her clodhoppers—but I guess I just don't think that the best way to start my job as the regional claims superintendent for Western States Insurance is to fork over $15,000,000 of the company's hard-earned money to a Nazi money-launderer, the male, Lebanese counterpart of Imelda Marcos, and an extortionate, blackmailing shyster with a candy-assed name like Eugene who embodies everything that I feel is currently wrong with this country.

I just ain't a-going to do it.

In the ringing words of Thomas Jefferson, "Millions for defense, not one penny for tribute."

Get to work.

Sincerely,
Pamela A. Holmstrum

)))

Craig D. Schaeffer
Attorney-at-Law
3615 Monterey
Palm Desert, CA

Ms. Pamela A. Holmstrum
Claims Superintendent
Western States Insurance Co.
801 Flower Street
Los Angeles, CA

4 August 1983

Dear Pamela A. Holmstrum,

Realizing now that you have recently emigrated from the unsullied moral purity of the prairie, I understand just how shocking and offensive you must find the corrupt stench of the former Bear Flag Republic. How awful it must be to emerge still fresh-faced and dewy-eyed from your white clapboard Methodist Church, hymnal clutched in your firm hand, to find that not all the world is as honest as the yeoman tillers of the land who were your plain, straight-shootin' kinfolk in Omaha.

Nevertheless, when in Sodom and Gommorah . . .

Pay the money, Pam. Pay it now. Without an eyewitness to this arson we are hosed.

You are a small insurance company. I am a small-time lawyer. And even Thomas Jefferson was never cross-examined by Eugene Petkovitch.

Sincerely,
Craig D. Schaeffer

P.S.: Doubtless you are a tall, blonde, blue-eyed right-wing Christian conservative who reads *National Review,* is a member of the NRA, voted for Reagan and sits around her house watching John Wayne videos. Am I right?

❭   ❭   ❭

Ms. Pamela A. Holmstrum
Claims Superintendent
Western States Insurance Co.
801 Flower Street
Los Angeles, CA

Craig D. Schaeffer
Attorney-at-Law
3615 Monterey
Palm Desert, CA

7 August 1983

Dear Craig,

Small is as small does.

Western States Insurance Company is small in the sense that it does not have $15,000,000 to give away. I'm afraid we are saving this money for foolish things like hurricanes, tornadoes, earthquakes, and accidental fires.

The question is: Are you a small lawyer? We need proof? Get proof. We need an eyewitness? Get an eyewitness.

Cheers,
Pamela

P.S.: As a matter of fact, I'm a short, brown-eyed brunette. Yes, I am a Methodist, no I am not a member of the NRA, and yes I voted for President Reagan. And yes, I do from time to time like to watch the Duke. You are probably short, have black hair, bottle-thick glasses, read *The New Republic,* are a member of the ACLU, voted for that loser Carter, and go to Woody Allen movies. Just curious.

P.P.S.: And it's Lincoln, not Omaha.

❯ ❯ ❯

Craig D. Schaeffer
Attorney-at-Law
3615 Monterey
Palm Desert, CA

Ms. Pamela A. Holmstrum
Claims Superintendent
Western States Insurance Co.
801 Flower Street
Los Angeles, CA

8 August 1983

Dear Pamela,

As the Muller household was built in a failing real-estate development, he had only one neighbor, a Mr. Nathan Silverstein. Mr. Silverstein is eighty-six years old and, when I contacted him in my initial investigation, claims to have seen "nothing—*bubkus*." Nevertheless I have tried to recontact Mr.

Silverstein but he does not seem to be in town. I
shall keep trying.

But I must still recommend that you lower your
testosterone level and settle this file.

Sincerely,
Craig

P.S.: Thank you for your characterization of me as
your stereotypical "Jew lawyer." Sorry to shatter
your dearly held illusions, but I am six-three, blue-
eyed with straight black hair. Yes, I am a Democrat,
a *proud* member of the ACLU, and voted against
Ronald Reagan numerous times. I liked Woody
Allen before he decided that he was Ingmar
Bergman.

❯ ❯ ❯

By Fax

Dear Craig,

If I get rid of some excess testosterone as you suggest, shall I
send it to you? Sounds like you could use some.

Pam

❯ ❯ ❯

By Fax

Dear Pam,

I am the Palm Desert triathlete champion in the 35–43 age
bracket.

Craig

❭ ❭ ❭

By Fax

Dear Craig,

I could run, swim, and bike you into the ground.

Pam

❭ ❭ ❭

By Fax

Pam,

Want to meet for lunch Monday and discuss it?

Craig

❭ ❭ ❭

By Fax

Craig,

You bet.

Pam

Chapter 11

OF COURSE I DIDN'T HAVE THE BENEFIT OF SEE-ing this epistolary yuppie romance until it was too late. Ditto the tapes that the testosteronally challenged—by Pam Holmstrum—Craig Schaeffer went out and got from Heinz Muller's telephone:

10 August. *From a tape made by Attorney Craig D. Schaeffer of a conversation between Heinz Muller (HM) and Amin Abdullah (AA).*

AA: Hello, Heinz?

HM: This is my home telephone.

AA: I know, this is why I called you here, okay?

   (Seventeen seconds of silence.)

AA: Hello? Hello?

HM: Did you take care of it?

AA: Take care of what?

HM: The old Jew.

AA: Sure, okay. I took care of it, okay?

HM: *Ja,* good. It's about time you did some—

AA: Don't worry, okay? I scared him off.

(Twenty-three seconds of silence.)

HM: You did *what?*

AA: I scared him away, okay? I called him up, told him maybe fire could happen at *his* house, you never know, okay? I told him—

HM: You are an idiot.

AA: No, I didn't call him an idiot, but I—

HM: No, I'm calling *you*—

AA: No, I'm calling you, remember, okay? Anyway, I don't think the old Jew ever is coming back.

HM: Idiot! Moron!

AA: Heinz, what's the matter, okay?

HM: You were not supposed to scare him off, you were supposed to *take care* of him.

AA: I thought we didn't like him.

HM: No, idiot. *Take care* of him.

(Thirty seconds of silence.)

AA: You mean *kill* him?

HM: I suppose I was trying to not actually say it.

AA: Heinz, you think the phone is bugged?

HM: No, the stupid Jew lawyer belongs to the ACLU.

AA: Heinz, when do we get the money, okay? The insurance company stopped sending me my checks and I'm getting low on cash, okay? And I lose bundle in casino just now, okay? Damn Vegas, I—

HM: You get the cash when you finish the job.

AA: Heinz, the house is burned to the ground, okay?

(Twelve seconds of silence.)

HM: The old Jew.

AA: You want me to burn *his* house to the ground?

(Fifteen seconds of silence.)

AA: Hello? Hello?

HM: The old Jew saw you leave the house when you set the fire, *ja*?

AA: I saw him looking out his window, okay?

HM: So he is a witness, *ja*?

AA: I guess so. It was dark, okay.

HM: If there is a witness to setting the fire, you won't get any money.

AA: Okay, okay.

HM: So you must take care of him.

AA: But Heinz, I scared him off, okay? I don't know where he is.

HM: I suppose this is my point, Sami.

AA: Ah.

HM: Sami.

AA: Yes, Heinz.

HM: Find the old Jew. Find Silverstein!

(Call terminated.)

Then there's this one, made on the same day I was cruising I-15 looking for Nathan myself:

14 August. *From a tape made by Attorney Craig D. Schaeffer, of a conversation between Heinz Muller (HM) and Amin Abdullah (AA), and an unidentified voice (UV).*

HM: *Ja*, hello.

AA: Heinz, hello.

HM: *Ja?*

AA: I'm driving on my way back from Vegas.

HM: Ja, good.

AA: Allah is good, Heinz, okay?

HM: If you say so, Sami.

AA: I see a car off the side of the road. I see an old man standing beside the car. I picked him up.

HM: This is fascinating, Sami.

AA: An old man, Heinz, okay? *An old man.*

(Ten seconds of silence.)

HM: An old man.

AA: An *old man*, okay?

HM: An old man.

AA: An old man. He's sitting here now.

HM: What old man?

(An unidentified voice in background of calling party:)

UV: Ask me who's on first?

AA: Not now, please. I'm talking on the phone.

UV: Ask me who's on first?!

AA: Who's on first, okay?

UV: Right.

AA: Right's on first.

UV: No, who's on first.

AA: That's what I ask you, okay? Who's on first?

HM: Hello? Hello? Sami?

AA: What?

UV: What's on second.

HM: Second? What? Who?

UV: No, who's on first.

AA: I don't know!

UV: Third base.

HM: What?!

UV: What's on second.

AA: It's the old man talking!

HM: Who?!

UV: Who's on first.

HM: What?

UV: What's on second.

AA: I don't know.

UV: Third base.

The tape goes on for quite some time but I think you get the idea. Judging by the timing of the tapes, it was about an hour later when Sami pulled off the road to let Nathan use the men's room.

Then:

HM: *Ja*, hello?

AA: Heinz, it's me.

HM: Where is the old man? Did you take care of him?

AA: Yes, he's in the men's room, okay?

HM: You left the body in the men's room?!

AA: No, he went by himself. Listen, Heinz, good news! The old man didn't recognize me so we don't have to kill him!

(Fifteen seconds of silence.)

HM: He's smarter than I thought. He is pretending not to recognize you.

AA: Why would he do that?

HM: So you don't kill him. They're clever, these old Jews.

AA: Not clever, Heinz—*crazy.* He keeps talking about sandwiches and naked ladies with birds and some guy named Mincemeat who knew Dali.

HM: Who?

AA: Please don't start that again, okay?

HM: You know what you have to do, Sami.

AA: I don't think it's necessary, Heinz.

HM: When did you start thinking, Sami? Do what you're told.

AA: Heinz, I have to hang up, okay? He's talking to someone.

(Call terminated.)

Chapter 12

GUESS WHO NATHAN WAS TALKING TO.

Bingo.

Of course, I didn't know about any of this when I rolled up and saw Nathan coming out of the men's room. I stopped the car, jumped out, ran over and . . .

Okay, I hugged him. It wasn't out of affection, mind you, it was from sheer relief.

After I finished hugging him, I held him at arm's length and yelled, "Where have you been?! I've been worried sick about you! I called the police, the hospital, the mor—"

"Did I tell you . . ."

"No jokes now, Nathan," I said. "Why did you take the car? Where have you been?"

"I—"

Nathan started to answer when a voice behind me said, "He's been with me, okay? He's okay, okay?"

He was a little guy, late thirties, curly black hair and big brown eyes. I couldn't quite place the accent, but it was Middle Eastern of some sort. He was wearing a ridiculous Hawaiian print shirt with a lot of flowers, white chinos and Gucci loafers with no socks.

"I picked him up," the guy continued, "and I'm giving him a ride home."

"I really appreciate that," I answered. "But I can take him from here."

The guy said, "I'm going his way, okay? No trouble. I live in Palm Desert."

"I'm going his way, too."

"Who are you?" the guy asked.

"Who am I?" I asked. "Who are *you*?"

You can take the boy out of New York . . . et cetera.

"Who are *you*?" the guy asked. "Mr. Silverstein, do you know this guy?"

"I—"

"He knows me," I said. "I sort of work for him. Come on, Nathan, let's go."

"Neal, you—"

"He doesn't have to go with you, okay?" the guy said. "He's going with me."

"I don't think so," I said.

"I do," he said.

Now this was a little guy. I figured even *I* could take him if I had to, and I'm no fighter. I have virtually none of the attributes of a good fighter: size, strength, speed, coordination or courage. And even I could have handled this guy.

Except for the gun.

A sleek little automatic that suddenly poked out of the ridiculous Hawaiian shirt and pressed into my stomach.

Did I mention I'm not especially courageous?

Now if you've seen a lot of private-eye movies or television shows, you'll know that this is the point where the hero gets a glinty cold look in his eye, then brings a lightning-quick karate chop down on the villain's wrist, knocking the gun to the ground. Then they struggle until the hero aims a punch to the villain's jaw and knocks him cold.

None of that happened. None of that happened because a) I am not especially courageous; and b) while it is true that there are no Nobel Prize committees waiting outside my door, neither am I a complete moron, popular opinion notwithstanding.

And while it is true that the hand is quicker than the eye, a bullet is quicker than either of them. So when someone shoves a gun into your tummy, you do several things: tremble, have an instant religious revelation, and sweat profusely. I guess that my whole life would also have passed before my eyes, but I was depressed enough already.

There's something else you do when someone shoves a gun into your tummy: You do what he says, which in this case was, "Get into the car, okay?"

As we were walking back to the car Nathan whispered to me, "I was trying to tell you."

"I know that now."

"You are the dumbest Irishman I have ever met."

"Shut up," the little guy hissed.

He put Nathan in the passenger seat then climbed into the back while he held the gun on Nathan and told me to drive.

I slid behind the wheel.

"Okay, drive," said the little guy.

"This is a standard shift," I said.

"Yes."

"I don't know how to drive a standard shift."

"I shoot you."

"It's true."

"I shoot you," he said. "Drive."

"Believe him," Nathan said. "He really is that stupid."

"I really am."

You could hear the little guy thinking about what to do. It seemed like he thought for a long time.

Then he said, "Drive or I shoot you."

I turned the key in the ignition. There was a horrible, metallic screeching noise. It was either the engine or the little guy's voice as he screamed, "This is a 1965 Mustang! It's very valuable!"

"Not for long," I said.

I cranked the engine again and stepped on a pedal or something.

"Nooooo!!!!" he screamed. "Okay, okay, okay, okay, okay, okay. *I* drive."

It took awhile for Nathan to climb into the backseat and me to slide into the passenger seat and Sami—as I later learned and you already know was his preferred alias—to climb into the driver's seat. Especially as Sami was trying to hold the gun on both of us while we were all doing what I would later come to refer to as the Lebanese Fire Drill.

But I began to feel a little better as I realized that Sami was not exactly Clyde Barrow when it came to being a gunslinger.

When we were all settled in, Sami said, "No funny business, okay?"

I think career criminals should be banned from watching old movies, don't you?

"No funny business," I said. "No monkey business either."

Then Sami seemed to being having difficulty figuring out how to shift, steer, and hold the gun in order to pull out of the rest stop. He simply didn't have enough hands.

"I'll hold the gun," I offered. "And if I try any funny business I promise I'll shoot myself."

But Sami apparently decided that the better option would be to stick the gun between his legs and expose himself to both the chance of emasculation and comments of a Freudian nature. So this is what he did, and pretty soon we were roaring west on Interstate 15.

For about a minute. Then he turned south onto a two-lane blacktop. The sign read, *Cima—East Mojave National Scenic Area.*

And even I had figured out by that point that Nathan had a definite reason for running away from Palm Desert and not wanting to go back, and that this reason was connected to the small but well-armed man now driving us somewhere for some reason I did not know.

Nathan turned in his seat to face me and said, "So Arthur says to the Irish kid, 'This isn't pastrami and . . .' "

I leaned over to Sami and said, "Shoot me."

Chapter 13

SAMI DIDN'T SHOOT ME.

As we headed further south into the bleakest terrain I have ever seen (and I have been to Bayonne, New Jersey), he just kept trying to interrupt Nathan's latest stream-of-semiconsciousness soliloquy with a persistent line of questioning.

"Do you recognize me?" Sami asked.

"So Arthur was laughing and— Sure I recognize you."

"Who am I?"

"Who are you?" Nathan asked. "You're the for-shit, *fekokteh*, no-goodnik who is kidnapping me, that's who you are. So Arthur—"

"I mean before that, okay?"

"Before what?"

"Before I kidnapped you, okay?" Sami asked. "Do you recognize me?"

"No," Nathan said. "I'm sorry, but I do not recognize you. I'm eighty-six years old, sometimes I don't recognize *me*. I look in the mirror and say, 'Who is this old man?' So, excuse me, I don't recognize me sometimes, I'm supposed to recognize you?"

Sami got an especially crafty look in his eye.

"Okay," he said. "So you don't recognize me as your . . . neighbor, for example?"

"And Arthur Minsky, who was a gentleman— What?"

"So you don't recognize me as your neighbor, for example?"

"Excuse me," Nathan said. "I live in a development that didn't get developed. What neighbors? I got no neighbors. What I got is a burned-up smelly mess next door. So, are you my neighbor?"

"No, no, no, no, no, okay?" Sami said. "That was just an example."

"Example of what?" Nathan shook a cigarette out of his pack and started to light it.

"Of how you might recognize me," Sami said. "Please don't smoke."

Nathan took a drag of the cigarette and went into his usual coughing spasm. When he was finished he said, "I *don't* recognize you."

"And," Sami said happily, "I don't recognize you."

"Must have been two other guys," I said.

Nobody laughed, so I said, "Having established that nobody recognizes anybody, why don't we just turn around, you can drop us back at the rest stop, and we'll all forget about the whole silly thing?"

This sounded like a very good idea to me. Especially because Sami now turned off the blacktop onto a dirt road. I have learned from long experience watching movies, that when a guy kidnaps you and takes you for a ride on a dirt road in a vast desert, you can cue the vultures.

And the smoke in the car was going to kill us all anyway.

"So what do you think?" I asked.

"I don't know what to think, okay?" Sami said. "I have to make a phone call."

"To tell you what to think?" I asked.

"Yes, okay?"

Sami punched some numbers on his portable phone. Being the ace private eye that I am, I memorized the number so that if I lived, I could get the name of the guy he was talking to.

"Hello, Heinz?" he said. There was a pause. "Okay, I'll stop using your name on the phone, Heinz, okay? . . . Yes, I still have him. Someone else, too. . . . You don't have to yell, Heinz. . . . Sorry, I forget. . . . Who else? Some younger guy, I don't know. Says he is working for the old man. . . . What? . . . Okay."

Sami turned to me. "Are you an insurance investigator?"

"No."

"He says he isn't, Heinz, okay? . . . Okay, I'll ask."

Sami turned to me again. "Do you know Craig Schaeffer?"

"No."

"He doesn't know him," Sami told Heinz.

"He says you're lying," Sami said to me.

"Who does?" I asked.

"He—" Sami said. "The person I'm talking with."

"I'm not lying."

Sami got back on the phone. "He says he's not lying, Heinz. . . . He's lying when he says that? . . . Okay, I'll ask."

"Are you a Jew?" Sami asked.

"Not that I'm aware of," I said.

It was a truthful response, seeing as how I was, to quote Smollett, "a love-begotten babe" and could only answer to half my lineage.

Nathan interrupted his soliloquy long enough to observe, "He's too stupid to be a Jew."

"He's not a Jew," Sami said into the phone.

"*I'm* a Jew," Nathan said.

"Heinz said that even if you were a Jew you'd lie about being one," Sami said to me.

"Okay," I answered. "I'm a Jew."

Nathan moaned.

"He *is* a Jew," Sami said happily.

"If he's a Jew," Nathan said, "I'm an Arab."

"*I'm* an Arab," Sami said.

"Of course," groaned Nathan.

"Good news, Heinz! The old man does not recognize me. I don't have to take care of him!" Sami said into the phone. "What? *Both* of them?"

Nathan said, "Of course. I get kidnapped by an Arab talking to a Nazi on the telephone."

"Both of them, Heinz?!"

Both of them *what*? I wondered. This didn't sound good.

"Both of them what?" I asked.

"I don't know about this, Heinz, okay?"

"Both of them *what*?!"

"We had a girl at Minsky's used to do an Arab routine," Nathan observed. "Not that she was an actual Arab, which she wasn't. She was a French Canadian. Name of Paulette something. Did a belly dance. Girl had a belly flat like a sheet of glass. Lovely girl. Used to go out with a fellow with a glass eye named Hannigan . . ."

I could have made him happy and asked what the name of the other eye was, but I was too concerned about Sami's conversation with Heinz. Sami's complexion at that moment looked a lot more Scandinavian than Semitic. He was ashen and blubbering, "I don't know about this, okay?" several times.

"I don't know about this, okay?"

"Let me talk to him," I suggested.

He didn't let me talk to him. He just said, "Yes, Heinz, I understand," and hung up the phone.

"What is it you understand, Sami?" I asked.

"What I understand," Sami said sadly, "is that I'm supposed to take care of you. Both of you, okay?"

"And by 'take care of,' " I said, "you mean . . ."

He nodded.

This time I went for the gun.

Chapter 14

Dear Diary,

What a day!

This afternoon I got on an airplane and flew to Palm Springs, California, to spend some time with Natty. I had forgotten what a sweet guy he really is! Natty may be old—and not exactly a firecracker, if you know what I mean—but he is a lot of laughs and at my age maybe the laughs are more important.

So I flew to Palm Springs and took a taxicab to Natty's condominium in Palm Desert.

What a place! It sits out in the middle of nowhere in the middle of the desert, and the first thing you see when you come through the gates is a waterfall! In fact, the whole complex—and how nice it's going to be when they finish it!—is called Desert Waterfalls. Isn't that cute? Where they get the water I don't know, but then again they have a lot of fountains in Las Vegas so I guess these people just know how to do these things.

I thought I'd surprise Natty, but guess what? Natty surprised me! He wasn't home! Maybe he stayed in Las Vegas for a couple of more days. If I know my Natty, he probably got snuggled up with some chorus girl but I'm not jealous. Good thing he told me where the key was!

Natty's place is very nice, as you would expect from someone with Natty's money. It sits right on the edge of a golf course and I wonder if Natty is worried about golf balls coming through his windows! He has a nice living room with a wonderful view of this golf course and the mountains on the other side. He has two bedrooms, so it will be "decent" for me to be there, as Natty says—as if at this age I'm worried about my reputation, but it is very sweet of Natty to be, don't you think?

All the furniture is white, which I think is very interesting, seeing as how my name is White. Maybe this was just meant to be.

And diary, there's even a piano!

The place is very clean and neat, which you would not expect from a widower, so I think Natty must have someone come in.

Natty's condominium sits at the end of the

street, so he doesn't really have any neighbors. There is an unfinished condominium across the street and the only one that is next door to Natty must have burned down. You can still smell the fire smell!

Oh, diary, I hope that Natty was sincere when he invited me to come and stay for a while and that it wasn't just sweet talk. Natty Silver could always talk a girl right out of her bloomers (blush, blush). But I think he really wants me to be here. I hope he is pleasantly surprised when he comes home and finds me here.

I was relieved to find out that even though Natty doesn't have neighbors he does have a lot of friends! I don't think that I was here more than half an hour—I barely had time to freshen up—when the visitors started to arrive!

First there was a nice young couple, Mr. Schaeffer and Miss Done, who wanted to talk with Natty. It was so funny, Diary! The young man asked if "Mr. Silverstein" was home.

I said, "You mean Natty?"

"Natty?" he said.

"Sure!" I said. "Natty Silver!"

You should have seen the smile on this fellow's face!

"Nathan Silverstein is Natty Silver!?" he asked.

"Sure!" I said.

I thought he was going to start jumping up and down, because it turns out that he is a big fan of Natty's. He started telling the young woman—who I guess had never heard of Natty (Where's she from, Diary, Kansas? Ha-ha.)—all about Natty's days in burlesque, and the old sketches, and lines from Natty's stand-up routines. This Schaeffer fellow even knew all those stinko beach movies that Natty was in with the boy with the hair and that girl with the bosom. You know, the one that used to be a mouse.

Well, the Schaeffer fellow was so excited that I took the liberty of inviting them in. (I hope Natty doesn't mind.) The Schaeffer fellow looked all around the place. He was so thrilled to see some of the mementos that Natty has!

"This is a picture of Natty with Phil Gold!" he said.

"I guess so," I said. Phil Gold was before my time.

"They say that Silver and Gold's 'Who's on First' was even better than Abbott and Costello's!" Schaeffer said.

Wait until Natty hears this!

"Don't get him started on the subject of Lou Costello," I said.

Well, Schaeffer would have looked around all day but the girl—and she was perfectly nice and polite—had business on her mind because she asked, "When will Mr. Silverstein be back?"

I said I didn't know but that I hoped it would be soon.

"Are you Mrs. Silverstein?" she asked.

"No, honey," I said. "There were at least three Mrs. Silversteins but I'm not one of them. I'm just a friend."

Then the boy seemed to realize that the girl wanted to conduct business because he started to talk in a deeper voice and said, "Will you have him telephone me the moment he gets back?"

Diary, I think that there's a spark between these two, if you know what I mean.

He handed me his card. I got a little concerned when I saw it because it said, Craig Schaeffer, Attorney-at-Law. I was afraid that I had made a mistake letting them in because maybe it was one of Natty's ex-wives trying to get more alimony.

So I started to say, "Mr. Schaeffer, if you are some kind of shyster here to try to bleed Natty dry, you can just—"

"No, no," he said quickly. "It's nothing like that. Mr. Silver might have seen something."

"Well, I'll ask him to call you."

"Thank you," said Schaeffer, and I could tell he didn't want to leave just yet.

Miss Done asked me, "By the way, were you here on the night of May thirtieth?"

"No, honey," I said. "I was working in Las Vegas."

The girl turned red so I added, "I play piano."

I mean, Diary, I may have accepted a lovely parting gift from time to time, but I will not let anyone mistake me for a common hooker.

So I sat down and started to play. I did "I Get a Kick Out of You," "I've Never Been In Love Before" and "What'll I Do" and they applauded and demanded an encore so I did "Adelaide's Lament," which they thought was very funny.

Diary, I must have sung two dozen songs and Schaeffer made tea and we all sang and had tea and chatted and then I said, "Natty must have some booze somewhere in this place." We found a fifth of Stoli and Schaeffer, made a pitcher of vodka martinis and we all sat out on the patio and had a nice cocktail.

After a while, the girl Pamela sat at the piano and sang "Fairest Lord Jesus" and she and I had a good cry. Guess what, Diary! She's a Methodist, too! From Nebraska, as it turns out. An old farm girl just like me!

Anyway, they finally had to go—a little tipsy, I think; young people these days just can't seem to hold their booze—and I was just about to see what was on television when the doorbell rang again.

This was a big fellow, even taller than Schaef-

fer and with muscles like a weight lifter. Short blond hair, blue eyes, chiseled jaw. Very handsome, if you go for that type.

And the accent, Diary! He talked like one of those Germans in the old movies.

"Izz Natan at hoom?" he asked.

"No, he's not," I said. "May I ask who is calling on him?"

He gave me what I'm sure he thought was a very charming smile.

"Yaah," he said. "I'm a frient of Natan's. I was driving by and saw lights and chust taught I't tropp in to zee how Natan is."

"Well, I'm sure he'll be back soon," I said.

Then he smiled kind of funny, Diary. As if he knew something that I didn't.

"Zen I koom pack latuh," he said. And left, just like that!

After he left I sat down and tried to think of what Nathan could have seen that a lawyer would want to talk to him about.

And where is Nathan, anyway? He certainly should be home by now.

Anyway, Diary, as soon as I find out the answers to these questions you can be assured that you'll be the first to know.

Your confidante,
Hope

Chapter 15

IT WAS A STUPID MOVE.

All the more so because I knew better. Even if I hadn't known that this sort of maneuver only works in the movies, I should have realized that a 1965 Mustang doing 80 mph on a dirt road does not respond well to life-and-death struggles between the driver and a passenger.

Anyway, I lunged between the seats and grabbed the pistol between Sami's legs. Sami grabbed my wrist, squeezed his legs and pulled back. His eyes were bugging out because the gun barrel was now pointed right at his balls and he was trying to control the car—and doing a pretty good job of it until Nathan took his cigarette and poked him in the eye.

"Ayyyiiiaaaaaa!" Sami screamed, and Nathan apparently admired the effect so much that he did it again.

"Ayyyyiiaaaaaaaaaaaaaa!"

So the next thing I knew the little car was doing 360s, Sami was screaming, Nathan was yelling, "How do you like that, you little Arab bastard?" and I was holding on to the gun handle in Sami's crotch and praying that the car wouldn't flip over and kill us all.

Which would have defeated the purpose of going for the gun in the first place.

I was pulling, Sami was screaming, Nathan was hollering, the car was spinning around, and then the gun went off.

Now Sami really screamed, because he thought his balls had been shot off. I screamed, too, because I thought the same thing. Then the gun went off again and we all screamed some more because the car plunged off the road. By the time it came to a landing, the gun ended up on the floor by Sami's feet, Sami was trying to get his pants off, I was clutching the back of the driver's seat, and Nathan was clutching his chest, gasping and coughing.

I lunged for the gun again but Sami had it in his hand and pointed it at my head. His hands were shaking like crazy but I figured that even he couldn't miss at this range so I sat back and tried to catch my breath.

Sami got out of the car and looked down at his pants.

"They're still there," he said. But he was hopping up and down because he had some truly wicked powder burns.

"What, were you trying to kill me?!" Nathan yelled at me.

"You tried to kill me!" Sami screeched at me.

So it was all my fault, of course. Then I saw two big holes in the floor of the car and realized that I had just shot not Sami but a 1965 Mustang. Then I smelled the gasoline.

"Get out!" I yelled at Nathan.

But he was struggling with the seat belt.

I jumped out the driver's side, ran around the back of the car and jerked the door open. These seat belts are perfectly simple when you're getting out at the grocery store or something, but they're another thing altogether when your hands are shaking, your legs are quivering, an old man is fumbling around with the latch, and the car is about to blow.

And the old man is smoking a cigarette.

I snatched the cigarette out of his mouth and tossed it. Then I got the latch unhooked, got my arms under Nathan's shoulders and knees and carried him away from the car. Sami realized what was going on and stopped hopping up and down long enough to start running.

Just as the stupid thing blew up.

Sami was hopping up and down again like Rumpelstiltskin, not because of the powder burns on his balls apparently, because now he was screeching, "My car! My car!"

I laid Nathan down, checked him for injuries and then felt around my own back to see if there were any stray pieces of a 1965 Mustang embedded in it. There weren't any, so it was with some relief that I sat down beside Nathan.

"My car, my car," Sami whimpered.

"Stop whining," I said. "You have insurance, don't you?"

For some reason that made Sami really moan. But by this time I was more pissed off than I was scared so I said, "Your precious car, my ass. You know something, you dumb little jerk? I'm glad I shot your car."

Sami pointed the gun at me. "I shoot you now!"

"You're not going to shoot us now," I said.

I looked around. On the other side of the road there was a smaller dirt road that led up behind a small knoll. It looked as if there were some deserted shacks up there. Maybe it was a deserted old mine. It would at least be some shelter for the night and some shade for the next day. If there was one.

I helped Nathan up and asked him if he was okay to walk. He said he was, so we started up the little road toward the shacks.

"I shoot you now!" Sami said as we headed out.

"No, you're not," I said. "Think for a second, Sami. If you shoot us now, you can't get away from the scene of the crime. If you shoot us now, you'll be a married man in San Quentin this time next year."

Sami had a wonderfully blank expression on his face that I would have thought was funny if we hadn't been marooned in the middle of the Mojave Desert with a not-overly-bright, incompetent criminal who still had the gun.

"Oh," Sami said.

"Oh," I answered.

"You're right," Sami said.

"This is probably a first for you," Nathan said, so I figured he was basically intact.

We reached the old shack, which was in fact the remnants of a played-out mine of some sort. It was a one-room cabin with two busted-out windows with no glass, flanking a doorway with no door. Not only was there no glass and no door, there was no water, no food, no blankets, no nothing of anything that we could use.

But there was nowhere else to go and Nathan looked like he was out of gas.

"I'm staying here," I said.

"Me too," said Nathan.

Sami didn't know what to do, so the next step was fairly predictable—he called Heinz.

"Mr. Silverstein," I whispered while Sami was dialing, "would you mind telling me why these people want to kill you?"

Nathan shrugged, "Maybe they saw the beach movies."

For some reason I thought he was being disingenuous.

Then again, I had seen the beach movies.

"Hello, Heinz?"

Nathan nudged me. "So this fella Hannigan had a schlong that a horse shouldn't have. That an elephant shouldn't have. They called him the One-Eyed Giant, and not because he was tall, either. . . ."

"Sorry, Heinz, I forget, okay? I'm very upset. . . . I can't do that, Heinz. . . . Because then I couldn't get away from the scene of the crime. . . ."

"One night we're in a restaurant," Nathan continued. "I'm having a nice piece of fish. Hannigan leans over the table to get the salt and his eye falls out. I go to cut my fish, think I'm looking at the fish-eye, but what I am looking at is Hannigan's eye. . . ."

"Can you come get me, Heinz? I'm sorry. I forget. Where am I? Hold on." Sami looked around. "In the desert."

"I start to cut into the fish," Nathan continued, "and Hannigan looks at me with his one eye and says, 'When did you ever see a fish with blue eyes?' Well, he starts to laugh, I start to laugh, Paulette starts to laugh. 'When did you ever see a fish with blue eyes?'

"Some old mine, or something. . . ." Sami started to give him directions. "Then you go . . . Hello? Hello?"

"The battery's dead," I said.

"Shit."

"You can recharge it in the car."

Sami gave me the best dirty look he could with his one good eye.

"I shoot you," he said.

"Not until Heinz gets here, you won't."

So I guess I told him.

"So Hannigan picks up his eye and goes into the washroom. I go with him. He starts to wash the eye under the tap when he loses his grip and the eye goes down the drain. We call the owner, Jack Donahue . . ."

"Heinz is coming," Sami said.

"Yippee."

". . . who was married to the former Dorothy DeLillo, whose sister was Marjorie DeLillo. Together they used to be the former DeLillo Sisters. . . ."

So Heinz was coming. At least we'd get to meet the whole brain trust. Heinz was coming, and I didn't expect Sami to try anything horrible until the boss got here. In the meantime there was a lot to do. It wouldn't hurt to get a fire going, because desert nights can get very cold, especially for an old man.

So I gathered up some slats from the old shack, borrowed Nathan's lighter, and got the fire going. Then I sat back on an old log, watched the fire, and the bright stars, which in the desert night looked like they were about ten feet away, and thought about old men and babies.

And lost chances.

Chapter 16

MAYBE IT *WAS* HORMONES.

But it just bugs me that whenever a woman gets truly emotional about something, men ascribe it to hormones. Like they're something we made up.

Hormones are real.

So is wanting a baby and wanting it *now*. I mean, I was no Suzy Creamcheese sorority chick when I met Neal. My biological clock was already ticking and if Neal wanted to wait two more years I just didn't think I could stand it. My biological clock was becoming a time bomb.

So if it was hormones, so what?

These hips were made for babies.

And the dumbshit would make a great father if he'd just get over his own screwed-up childhood, and he knows it. But I guess I was a little rough on him. Anyway, after I talked to him on the phone I went upstairs and checked the calendar, did the temperature thing, and discovered that the old ovaries were in overdrive.

We're talking prime time.

And I thought, hell, if I can get my butt down to Palm Desert maybe I could surprise Neal and we could do it before he had a chance to start whining about how screwed-up he is.

So I phoned up Peggy Milkovsky and she phoned up one of the crop-spraying outfits and sure enough there was a pilot heading down to Indio, which isn't too far from Palm Desert, and he said he'd be happy for the company.

I put a few things in a bag, met the pilot at the airstrip and got to Indio just as the sun was going down. I found Nathan Silverstein's address in the Greater Coachella Valley phone book, got myself a cab over there and rang the bell.

To tell the truth, I felt kind of pathetic standing there on the front step, with my bag, my bubbling ovaries, and my round heels. Talk about easy.

Chalk it up to temporary insanity, please.

A woman answered the door. I think she was expecting somebody else because she was wearing a white see-through full-length negligee, high heels, and red lipstick.

"You must be Hope White," I said.

"That's right, honey," she said. She gave me a woman's once-over and added, "And Nathan must be doing better than I thought."

"Is Neal Carey here, by any chance?"

"No, he's not."

Then I did the weirdest thing.

I started to cry. I don't mean sniffle, either. I started to bawl.

I'm no wussy. I'm a rootin', tootin' cowgirl mountain woman. I've birthed calves, gelded horses, and stitched up drunken cowboys. I've comforted abused kids, stuck shotgun barrels into the crotches of their no-good daddies, even listened to Neal Carey try to sing and never cried. I don't cry easily.

But there I was, standing in front of a nearly naked woman bawling my eyes out and I don't know why.

It's just that at that moment I really needed to see him and he wasn't there.

So I was weeping and Hope White pulled me inside and sat me on on the couch and actually said, "There, there, dear . . ."

I was just blubbering.

"You're looking for Neal?" she said gently.

I blubbered and nodded.

"You really need to find him, don't you?"

Blubber and nod.

"Honey," Hope said as she put her arm around me, "are you crying because this Neal got you into trouble?"

"No," I blurted, "I'm crying because he didn't!"

Next thing I knew my head was resting in her ample bosom and she was stroking my hair and saying, "There, there. . . . There, there. . . . You just cry and tell Hope all about it."

And I did.

Chapter 17

Dear Diary,

What a night!

After the German fellow left I took a long bubble bath, made myself some dinner out of Natty's refrigerator, then got all dressed up the way Natty likes. (Blush, blush.)

Sure enough, about an hour later the doorbell rang and I thought it was Natty and he had forgot his key. So I went to the door, flung it open, flung my arms open to show him (blush, blush) the goods, and Surprise! *It was a young woman!*

At first I was a little upset, Diary, because I thought Natty had himself some young honey and let me tell you, this one is a looker! Thick black hair, gorgeous eyes, and the hips . . .

Well, it turns out that she's not looking for

Natty after all (A good thing for her. A good thing for Natty!), but for this Neal Carey I met in Vegas. The one who was supposed to be bringing Natty home.

I told the poor dear—Karen is her name—that Neal wasn't there and the the sweet thing starts to cry like her heart is going to break. What else could I do? I brought her in and sat her down and listened to her story.

Diary, the trouble is that this Neal will marry her but not give her a baby. Just the reverse of the usual story. Go figure.

I told her, "Sweetie, you're going about this all the wrong way!"

"What do you mean?" she asked.

I told her, "Just get him in the sack but don't tell him that you 'forgot' your birth control."

"I couldn't do that," she said. "It wouldn't be honest. It wouldn't be healthy for the relationship."

Honesty, relationship . . . *Young people these days. In our day we didn't worry so much about honesty and relationships. Girls got pregnant, guys married them, we had families, we made out all right.*

Anyway she had a good cry and told me all about her and Neal. Imagine that boy not wanting to have a baby with a beautiful girl like this!

But then we got to wondering, Where were

Natty and Neal, anyway? When Karen told me about Natty taking Neal's car and Neal setting off to find him, I started to get real worried. Then I told Karen about Mr. Schaeffer and Miss Done, and the German fellow, and she started to get concerned.

Then Karen called Mr. Graham, and I got on the extension, and the three of started to get worried together.

What could Natty have seen? we all wondered.

"Unless it had something to do with the fire," I said.

"What fire?" Mr. Graham asked.

"The one next door," I said.

"Do you happen to know the address?" Mr. Graham asked.

"I can go look," I said, and I did. The street numbers are painted on the sidewalks. It was 1385 Hopalong Way, and I told Mr. Graham so.

He said he'd call back. In the meantime Karen tried to call Mr. Schaeffer, but he wasn't in. She found his home phone number but he wasn't there, either. I'll just bet he's out with Miss Done. There's a spark there, I think.

Mr. Graham called back half an hour later.

"The condo belongs to a Heinz Muller," he said.

Diary, that's the German fellow who said he

was Natty's friend! I should have known that Natty wouldn't be friends with a German. He won't even ride in a German-made car! What was I thinking about?!

Suddenly, Diary, I knew what had happened! Natty had seen something in connection with the fire! After all, Natty had spent years playing the Catskill hotels—he'd know arson when he saw it.

I think—Oh, excuse me, Diary! There's the door! It must be Natty! Thank God! I'll be right back!

Chapter 18

From the tape of an illegal microphone planted at the Silverstein residence by Craig Schaeffer. The voices have since been identified as those of Heinz Muller (HM), Hope White (HW) and Karen Hawley (KH).

HW: Just what do you mean, coming in like that? How did you get in?

HM: What did the old Jew tell you?

HW: I beg your pardon? "Old Jew"? You get out right now before I telephone the police.

HM: What did he tell you?!

HW: Let go of me!

HM: What did he tell you?!

HW: Nothing.

(Sound of a slap.)

(Sound of footsteps.)

KH: Just what the hell do you think you're doing?! Let her go! Then get your sorry butt out of here before I kick it out.

HM: You terrify me.

KH: Mister, I'll put this boot so far up your ass you'll need a pair of vise-grips and a bottle of good whiskey to get it out.

HM *(Laughing)*: I would like to see you try.

(Unidentified sound: a dull thump.)

(Various bellowing sounds.)

KH: Hope, call 911.

HW: Honey, I haven't seen a kick like that since the line at Harrah's.

KH: Hope, call 911.

HM: Don't do that.

(Sound of telephone ringing.)

HW: Silverstein residence. Oh, hello, Mr. Graham. Listen, I think we've located Mr. Muller. He's here right now and— Oh, dear, I'm afraid I have to hang up right now. He has a—

Chapter 19

GUN.

I should have known.

I mean, I kicked that son of a bitch between the legs so hard I half expected to see his balls come flying out his mouth. The big muscle-bound Kraut hollered like a bull that's becoming a steer. Neal would probably call this an "apt analogy" because— Well, never mind. You get the picture.

And Neal is always telling me that if I'm going to put a guy down make sure he *stays* down. You know, finish him off. "Turn out the lights, the party's over" kind of thing.

As if Neal would know. The last time I saw him fight was a barroom brawl with some white-supremacist trash a couple of years back. Neal blocked a couple of punches with his jaw and then kind of dragged his guy to the floor and passed out on top of him. He wasn't exactly John Wayne. But he was game.

I think fighting's stupid, anyway.

It was just that this Muller jerk was so damn arrogant. You know, first he breaks in, then he pushes Hope around, and I've just seen enough of that trashy behavior to last a lifetime.

And I gave him a chance. I explicitly told him what would happen if he didn't leave and he said he'd like to see me try it, and I was happy to oblige him in that particular request.

He was one big, strong, hulking side of beef, too. But every man has his Achilles' heel, you know, and generally it isn't anywhere near his foot. I mean if you've ever seen a cowboy chasing a little calf, and that calf kicks a hoof back around crotch-high, and you've seen that cowboy kneeling in the dirt sucking for air, you have a pretty good idea of what Heinz-baby looked like at that particular moment.

So, anyway, there he was on his knees with his big baby-blues bulging out his stupid face, and that's where I ought to have finished him off, according to famed pugilist Neal Carey. But I didn't and the son of a bitch had a gun.

A big pistol. A magnum.

I have a theory about men who own magnums. My theory is that they have to buy one because they don't have one, you know? And the way this Muller galumph held that handpiece, you just got the feeling that however large he was elsewhere . . . well, the big pistol was by way of compensation.

And they talk about *us* and hormones.

So this Muller turd pulls this gun and says, "This is a .57 magnum and could blow your head off. So do what I say."

So I said, "Okay, Heinz-57. You got the gun, big boy, what do you want us to do?"

"What do you know?"

I felt like I was Dustin Hoffman in that movie with Laurence Olivier—you know the one where old Larry's the Nazi dentist—because I don't know anything except that maybe Heinz-57 burned his own house down and maybe Silverstein saw him do it, but I didn't think that was exactly the brightest thing in the world to say at that particular moment.

"I know that you burned your house down and that Natty saw you," Hope piped up.

She really is a lovely person, but you don't want her holding your money in a poker game, if you know what I mean.

Heinz-57's eyes lit up like a pinball machine, as if this news actually made him happy. There are some jamokes, you know, who are just looking for a rationale to hurt people, and I think that old Heinz-57 was one of these characters.

So he herded us outside where he had his Land Rover parked.

A brand-new Land Rover. I guess arson pays.

142

He starts to put me in the driver's seat, then asks, "Do you know how to operate a standard shift?"

"Heinz-57, I could *build* a standard shift."

I didn't bother to tell him that I grew up on a ranch that had a lot more tumbleweed than money on it, so I'd helped my father reconstruct an old flipped-over H tractor about three hundred and thirty times and did more than just hold the wrench, too.

Could I operate a standard shift. About the only person I knew in central Nevada who couldn't operate a standard shift was Neal, and God knows I tried to teach him.

The man is just hell on cars.

So I got behind the wheel and Hope sat in the passenger seat. Heinz-57 sat behind me with his magnum (the pistol, that is) poked behind Hope's ear.

"No monkey business," he said. "Do not even consider blinking the lights, or speeding, or driving to a police station. I will blow her head off."

This was a pretty smart threat. He knew he couldn't blow my brains out or the car would crash.

"Where are we going?" I asked.

"I will give you directions," he said. Then added, because he just couldn't help being an asshole, "We are going to meet some Jews in the desert."

Jews in the desert. There's a fresh concept.

But I figured that one of those Jews was probably Nathan. And I was praying that the other one was Neal.

Chapter 20

AH, NIGHT IN THE DESERT.

The open sky, the sparkling stars, a fire crackling in the brisk air.

Add to these simple pleasures the joys of no food, no water, no blankets, the inimitable camaraderie of an old man soliloquizing about the good old days, and a moronic Lebanese kidnapper pointing a gun at you, and the heightened sensibilities produced by the awareness of one's imminent execution, and you have yourself one of life's peak experiences.

It's Miller time!

Nathan seemed to occupy a mental space all his own. I could hardly blame him. A man his age must have been exhausted after a carjacking, a kidnapping, a car accident, an explosion and a hike up a dirt road to an abandoned mine where he would be starved, dehydrated and frozen. I didn't feel so zippy myself.

So it was little wonder that he had gone into the drone zone, a stream of consciousness that had innumerable pools and eddies.

We all leaned against our logs and stared into the fire. Sami held the gun in his lap pointed directly at yours truly while he used his free hand to alternately massage his sore crotch and rub his inflamed eye.

Nathan had been at it for a good two hours and had just worked his discursive way back to the DeLillo Sisters.

I was barely listening as Nathan droned. ". . . and the DeLillo Sisters were twins. You could not tell them apart except that Dorothy DeLillo had a mole on her *tukus*, but of course only Donahue knew this because the DeLillo Sisters were in vaudeville, not burlesque. Nobody saw Dorothy DeLillo's *tukus* except for Donahue because Dorothy DeLillo was very proper except for one time, and that was when she shared a bill with the Great Rulenska. Hypnotists always have Russian names, don't ask me why. But you never see a hypnotist with an Italian name. Rulenska wasn't Russian, he was Polish, from New Britain, Connecticut. Why they call this town New Britain I'll never know because it's all Polacks there. I stayed one night in New Britain on my way from New Haven to the Catskills. . . ."

There go the DeLillo Sisters, I thought. And I still didn't know what had happened to Hannigan's glass eye, either. Not to mention how Nathan had come to teach "Who's on First" to Lou Costello.

I looked over at Sami, who had a dazed look in the one eye that wasn't all red and swollen and rapidly closing.

". . . because there was a snowstorm. You cannot get a lightbulb changed in New Britain, Connecticut, because there are so many Polacks living there. No Jews either, so just try to get decent deli. A Polish sausage maybe. Sauerkraut, *drech*.

"In the Catskills they have Jews. More Jews in the Catskills than in Israel. I played the Catskills many times. The delicatessen? Magnificent. Not Wolff's perhaps, but very good. The one time I played the Catskills after spending an endless night in New Britain, Connecticut, I do my schtick to an empty room. There are maybe twelve Jews plus the waiters in the room. Try making twelve Jews and three waiters who are making no money laugh. They laugh at nothing. A fire maybe they laugh at, because the hotel is losing so much money.

"I told them the joke about the priest and the rabbi. Father Murphy goes up to Rabbi Solomon and says, 'Sorry about the fire in your synagogue.' Solomon says, 'Shhh. It's tomorrow.'

"Nobody laughed. To them this is not funny. That night, what do you think? I can't get to sleep, I look out the window of my room, what do I see?"

Nathan had my attention. It finally occurred to me (duh) that what I was hearing was what we graduate-school types recognize as an allegory. Sami, on the other hand, was not really listening, but I don't think he ever had the advantage of attending graduate school. So he was just staring into the fire. But trained as I am to find symbolism in everything, whether it's there or not, I was listening, as they say, intently.

"I see Sammy Stein, the hotel owner, sneaking out the back of the restaurant with the gasoline cans. Sammy looks up and sees me. Then he gets into his car and a few minutes later, guess what? The restaurant burns down. I don't say anything, I mind my own business. What am I going to do, testify?

"A few days later Sammy, that schmuck, calls me, tells me to keep my mouth shut if I know what's good for me. I decide to go work Vegas for a while. In Vegas, I have friends."

"What happened with the DeLillo Sisters?" I asked softly.

"Ah," Nathan said. "Dorothy DeLillo's mole remained just a rumor until there is a party at Donovan's afterhours. Everybody wants to see the mole! In a nice way, I mean. Very friendly. Dorothy refuses. Finally Rulenska says, 'I can make you show the mole.' Dorothy says, 'Bullfeathers. I have seen your crummy act a hundred times, it's a phony.' Rulenska just laughs, gets out his big pocketwatch and starts to chant, 'Watch the watch, watch the watch,' over and over again.' "

Nathan was moving his index finger back and forth across his face.

" 'Watch the watch, watch the watch.' 'You're getting sleepy, sleeeepy, sleeeeepy, sleeeeeeeeeepy . . .' "

Sami's good eye was just about closed. His chin touched his chest.

"Sleeeeeeeeepy . . . sleeeeeeeeeeepy . . . sleeeee-eeeeeeeeepy . . ."

I went for him.

Sami opened his eyes and raised the gun.

I punched him in the face.

A knockout.

Chapter 21

YEAH, OKAY, HE WAS FIVE-THREE, ALREADY prone, and had previous wounds, but it was still a knock-out.

I grabbed the gun from his limp hand.

"A regular Benny Leonard you are," Nathan said.

I got into the spirit of camaraderie and said, "A regular Rulenska you are."

After all, Nathan and I had teamed up to the get the gun. Me with my lightning moves, he with his hypnotist memories.

"There was no Rulenska, you stupid," Nathan said. "I made it up."

"Bullfeathers."

"The *emmis.*"

I looked down at Sami's unconscious body.

"What are we going to do with him?" I asked.

"Shoot him."

"We can't just shoot him, Nathan."

"Why not?" Nathan asked. "He was going to shoot us."

This was true. It was also true that Heinz was probably still planning on it. But that was another discussion.

"We don't have anything to tie him up with," I said. I didn't want to take a chance on getting that close to Sami anyway. I wasn't all that confident about my chances for another stunning knockout. "Let's just leave him where he is and keep the gun on him."

"Simpler to shoot him," Nathan said. "You want I should do it?"

"No."

"I could poke his other eye," Nathan offered.

"You're a vicious old man."

"After what he's put me through?"

Then he told me about seeing Sami come out of the house with gasoline cans and drive off. How he thought that Sami saw him. How Sami had called him and threatened to kill him and how he had run off to Vegas.

"Is that why you kept stalling?" I asked. "Why you took the car?"

"An Einstein, this boy is."

"Why didn't you just tell me?"

"I thought you were with the insurance company," Nathan said. "That you were going to make me testify."

"But why get in Sami's car?"

"What was I going to do? Run?" Nathan asked. "I had almost escaped at the men's room when you stopped me. Schlemiel. You are dumber maybe than Lou Costello, who did not know salami from pastrami."

"True," I said, "but I have a wicked punch."

"What wicked punch?" he asked. "You knocked a sleeping man unconscious. My grandmother could have made that punch and she's been dead forty years!"

"Yeah, but he had a gun," I pointed out.

"He was asleep!" Nathan yelled. "I put him to sleep! What more did you want, I should maybe put a gas mask on his nose, then you could punch him? I should tie up the sleeping man first, maybe? Then you could be a hero and punch the sleeping man?!"

I said, "He was clearly awake before I— It was Lou Costello who brought the salami sandwich to Arthur Minsky?"

Nathan raised his arms, "What do you think I've been trying to tell you?!"

Sami woke up. He lifted his head and moaned, "Don't hit me anymore, okay?"

"Don't hypnotize you, you mean," Nathan said.

Sami rubbed his head and looked around. He saw the gun in my hand.

"Heinz isn't going to like this," he said.

"Who is Heinz, anyway?" I asked.

"A Nazi," Nathan said.

"A Nazi?" I asked. "Do you know this guy?

"Who needs to know him?" Nathan asked. "With a name like Heinz? Nazi!"

"That doesn't necessarily—"

"He is," Sami said.

"Is what?" I asked.

"A Nazi," Sami said.

"Aha!" said Nathan.

"And he sent you to kill Nathan?" I asked.

"It's true," Sami admitted.

"A Nazi and an Arab want to kill a Jew," Nathan said. "So what's new?"

"And he's coming here to pick you up?"

Sami said, "After I dump your bodies."

"And you were willing to do all of this for an insurance claim?!" And I thought *I* was cynical.

Sami shook his head. "Not for the insurance money, okay? For the lawsuit."

"I don't get it."

"Heinz figured it out," Sami said. "What he planned, okay, was to burn down the condo and leave enough clues so that the insurance company would deny the claim because of arson, but not enough evidence that a jury would decide arson. So you sue the insurance company and the jury gives you millions in puny damages."

"Punitive damages," I said.

"Okay," Sami said.

"And that works?!"

"Oh, yes," Sami said solemnly. "Heinz has done it many times, okay?"

"I love this country," I said.

"Me too," said Sami. "Of course, witnesses are not good, okay?"

"I wasn't going to be a witness!" Nathan yelled.

Sami asked, "Who knew?"

"Ask," Nathan snapped. "I would have told you."

Sami shrugged.

"I assume Heinz owns a gun," I said.

"A big one."

"Will he come alone?"

"Heinz has no friends," said Sami. "Except me, okay?"

"Sami," I said. "You're not Heinz's friend anymore, okay? You're our friend, okay?"

"Okay."

"Do you know why this is?" I asked.

It was a rhetorical question, but Sami answered, "Because you have the gun, okay?"

I guess if you grow up in Beirut you have a firm grasp of the dynamics of friendship.

"Because I *will* shoot you," I said, "if you try to double-cross us."

I can't believe I said that. And yes, I am embarrassed about it. I'm embarrassed for two reasons: One; it's a tired old line from about thirty-seven bad movies. Two; of course he was going to try to double-cross us.

"No, no, no, no, no," Sami said. "*We're* the friends now, okay?"

As an expression of unabashed duplicity, Henry Kissinger couldn't have it said it better.

"So you're going to do exactly what I tell you to do, right?" I said to Sami.

"You bet," Sami said. "What do you want me to do?"

I tried to maintain some vestige of authority as I said, "I don't know yet. But when I *do* know, I want you to do whatever it is."

With that ringing declaration we settled in to wait for Heinz. Not that it was necessarily a given that Heinz would get there first. I hadn't checked in with Graham, and knowing him like I do, he'd have already started to track me down.

Chapter 22

I FIGURED OUT THAT WE WERE IN A SORT OF RACE in reverse. That is, the longer it took me to chauffeur Heinz-57 to wherever it was we were going, the more time I'd give Joe Graham to get someone there first.

Did you get that?

The point is that I lightened up considerably on my normal lead foot.

See, where I live, Austin, Nevada, is in the middle of your wide-open spaces. In fact they call Route 50, which stretches across Nevada into Utah, "The Loneliest Highway in America," and we tend to look at the speed limit more as a suggestion than a command. I've never gotten a speeding ticket. In fact I don't even know anyone who's ever gotten a speeding ticket.

So I normally drive pretty fast but now I slowed down,

thinking that "55 Saves Lives" might be pretty literal in this case.

Heinz-57 caught right on.

"You are driving slow," he said.

"I'm doing the limit."

"Faster."

"You told me not to speed."

He thought about this for a second, then said, "Speed cleverly."

"It ain't the autobahn, you know."

"Step on it."

I don't know where he got the "Step on it" bit, but I took him at his word and put that pedal to the floor.

It had nice pickup for a four-wheeler.

"What are you trying to do?!" he yelled.

"Follow instructions!"

"You wish for the police to stop us?!"

Well, yes, bonehead. That's what I had in mind as long as you gave me permission. I didn't say that, of course.

Anyway, he yelled, "Slow down!"

"Make up your mind."

Then Heinz-57 got on the phone and started punching numbers.

"Don't listen," he ordered.

"What did you say?" I asked.

"He said not to listen," Hope answered helpfully.

"I didn't hear him," I said. "I wasn't listening."

There was something in me that loved jerking Heinz-57's chain. Maybe it was the hormones.

It didn't matter, though, because the other party didn't answer. I could hear that mousy little voice on the other end say, "The mobile phone customer you are trying to reach is not answering. Please hang up and try later." As if it's any of their business. I mean if I want to sit there and let that phone ring until Alexander damn Graham Bell gets up and answers it, I will.

Heinz-57 wasn't all that thrilled either. I glanced in the rearview mirror and saw that he had this bewildered, confused look on his puss. You know, that sort of dazed expression that Type Triple-A anal retentives get when things aren't going exactly the way they planned.

I made Heinz-57 out to be one of those kind of cooks who absolutely, positively cannot substitute an ingredient in a recipe. There are some people like that, you know. They have everything together and are just paragons of control until they find out they have to use Monterey Jack instead of cheddar and then they just go to pieces.

I filed this piece of psychological insight away, figuring it might be useful at some point, because it was clear just then that Heinz-57 had just had to swallow his first slice of cheddar. (I guess Neal would call that a "tortured metaphor" but screw him.) Whoever it was that old Heinzy was calling, he damn well expected him to be there. And the fact that it was a mobile phone led me to believe that Heinzy was not precisely sure where he was going.

This would, of course, drive a Type Triple-A anal retentive German (Neal would call this a "double redundancy" but screw him again) just nuts.

"Not home, huh?" I said.

See, I'm one of those kind of cooks who just can't resist squirting lighter fluid on the charcoal briquettes.

"I told you not to listen!"

"What's that?"

"I told you not to listen!"

"Sorry?"

"He told you not to listen, sweetie."

"I told you not to listen!!"

"Yeah? And what are you going to do about it?" I asked. You know, lighter fluid, briquettes. Hormones, whatever.

He sat back and sulked for a minute. Then he said, "When we get to the desert you will see what happens."

"We're *in* the desert, dickhead."

"Language, sweetie."

"Sorry."

"Into the Mojave," Heinz specified. "Where your bodies will never be found."

"Sorry?" I said. "What did you say? I wasn't listening."

But I sure as hell was. Old Heinz-57 was taking us up to the Mojave, where the sun could kill you in about forty-five minutes. That is, if Heinz-57 didn't want the giggles of shooting us. And he was right—either way, nobody would ever find our bodies. Not mine, not Hope's, not Nathan's, not Neal's.

Neal—the reluctant father of our unconceived child.

Then a really awful thought occurred to me. If Heinz-57 was planning to dump our bodies, had he already dumped Nathan's?

And Neal's?

Chapter 23

I WAS TRYING TO STAY AWAKE.

You'd have thought it would be easy, right? What with the fear, anxiety, hunger and thirst and all. But there's something in the human system that just wants to shut down when things get too hideous, and I was struggling to stay conscious and keep that gun pointed right between the beady eyes of our new friend Sami.

So I tried to think about things.

First I tried to focus on the dynamics of our situation. Heinz was on his way and had a gun. Heinz would be thinking that we were already dead and all he had to do is pick up Sami and drive back. So the thing to do was to hide, throw Sami out as bait, and get the drop—oh God, did I say "get the drop"?—on Heinz before he figured out that we weren't dead.

Simple, right? What could go wrong?

Another possibility was that Graham would track us down before Heinz could. It wasn't out of the question. Graham wouldn't fly out—that would waste time—but he'd direct efforts over the phone. He would have already used my credit-card number to get the car-rental agency and the license plate of the car. A little grease would have the state police locate the car at the rest stop. That's where it would get tricky. Would they just assume we kept going west on Route 15, or would they think of taking the back road south through the Mojave? If they looked down the back road, they'd see the wreck of the car and figure it out from there. If not . . . hello, Heinz.

So what would Graham do? Send his troops on the highway or the back road?

Easy. Graham would do both.

Graham would have a map spread out in front of him and would consider each and every possible route from where they found the rental car. Then he'd send his troops out on a coordinated, organized search with designated check-in times and places.

You'd have to know Graham to know how sure I was of this. For example, this is a man who does his weekly grocery shopping as follows: He decides what he's going to cook, then writes down all the ingredients he needs. Then he redoes that list, rewriting the items in the order they appear in the grocery store as you work from the left aisle to the right. That way he can go through the store once, in one smooth progression from left to right.

If any man could sit behind a telephone in New York

City and find the splotch of a burned-out car in the middle of the Mojave Desert, that man was Joe Graham.

Since I figured it was a push between Heinz and Graham getting there first and there was nothing I could do to affect the results of that race, I moved on to another topic.

Babies.

Specifically, *a* baby. Karen's and mine. Not a real baby, not yet, but a putative baby. A possible baby.

Baby, baby, baby, baby. Just the word was intimidating, and yet . . .

Maybe it was the very real prospect of imminent death that made me reconsider my timetable on the *b*-word thing. Two years *was* a long time and a lot of things could happen. And it would seem like a waste if Karen and I didn't have a . . . a kid. Karen would be a terrific mother and I would be a—well, I could be an acceptable father.

There probably was something to all Karen's psychobabble about unresolved rage at my absent father and inadequate mother. That didn't necessarily mean that I couldn't rise above it, though. A man plays the cards he's dealt, right?

A man. Sigh. A father.

Now if there's a scarier word than "baby", it's "father".

I know it seems obvious to you, but I just then figured out that it wasn't the kid I was so afraid of, it was being the kid's father. I mean, what does a father actually do? I knew from watching old television shows that a father takes the kid into the study and says wise things to it, but that was about the extent of my knowledge. And I believe we've already pretty much established that I don't exactly overflow with wisdom. What was I supposed to do, take the kid into the study and say petulant things to it?

Oh, man. A father. Sigh.

Okay, so I never knew my father. I never even knew who he was. For the longest time as a kid I thought he was Chinese or something, because when I asked my mother who my father was she answered "some John".

In my childhood years, such as they were, Some John had loomed large in my imagination. He was variously a football player, a baseball player, an astronaut, a war hero—you get the pathetic idea—and in my imagination he was always coming back for me. Somehow he'd get the idea that he had a kid and would move heaven and earth to track me down, and one day I'd be sitting on the fire escape and see him coming down the alley and he'd look up and see me and just *know,* and in that deep, manly television voice he'd say, "Son, thank God I found you."

Pathetic, huh?

When I got a little older, say ten, I gave that one up. By that time I figured out that my father was just another pathetic loser who had to pay a woman to be with him. The kind of guy that, even if he knew he had a kid out there somewhere, wouldn't give a good goddamn.

So what does a father actually do? See, I can't tell you. I can only tell you what my father actually did.

Nothing, that's what.

So what chilled me right then, more than even the freezing desert air, was the unavoidable fact that at least half of me was that guy, that bum. And I didn't want to do to any kid what . . .

Man, talk about bathetic.

Next topic.

An old man. Nathan.

I was worried about him. He was shivering now, even by the fire, and I didn't know how much more he could take, ornery as he was. He'd already been through a lot, and who knew what was coming up?

I snuck a glance at him. He was lying with his head propped against the log, his blue eyes were watery and tired-looking now. He seemed small and frail.

And quiet.

Not pouting-quiet, either, but really quiet. For the first time since I'd known Nathan, he was truly silent.

I guess old men look at death all the time.

"Hey, Nathan?"

"Yeah?"

"Who's on first?"

We went through almost the whole routine before he fell asleep. Then I managed to slip an arm under him and hold him against my chest.

It was still cold but that might keep him a little warmer.

Me, too, I guess.

Chapter 24

ONE THING ABOUT THE DESERT—YOU CAN HEAR a car coming from a long way off.

The sun was just up, a pale orange circle in a lavender sky. That wouldn't last long. Soon the sun would be blazing, washing out the sky to a blue so pale it's almost white.

Nathan and Sami were asleep. I eased my arm from under Nathan, got up, and peeked over the edge of the knoll. A car was coming up from the south. I figured we had about ten minutes.

When I came back to the fire, Nathan's eyes were open. For a second there I thought I saw Nathan smile.

I put an ungentle toe into Sami's foot.

"Wake up," I said. "What kind of car does Heinz have?"

"He has a Mercedes," Sami mumbled.

That was good news. I wasn't sure what a Mercedes

was. I had in mind a sleek sedan, though. The car I saw looked more like a small truck.

"And a Porsche, a BMW, and a Land Rover," Sami said.

That was bad news. The car I had seen looked like it could be a Land Rover.

"What color's the Land Rover?" I asked.

"White."

"I think Heinz is here," I said. "Okay, friend Sami, you know what to do?"

Sami bobbed his head like one of those dogs in the back window of a car. "I tell Heinz your bodies are in the shack. I bring him in, okay?"

"Okay," I said. "And you do anything different, I'm going to put one in your back."

I'd heard this line in a movie and thought it sounded pretty tough. Yeah, okay, I thought that Sami would think it was pretty tough. He didn't exactly quake, though, so I added, "If you try to signal him in any way, any funny faces, any hand gestures, anything at all, I'll blow your head off."

"Okay, okay," Sami said. "We're the friends now."

"Yeah, we're the friends."

Then I heard the crunch of tires on gravel. The car was coming up the dirt road.

"Places, please, gentlemen," I said. I helped Nathan into the shack and sat him down on the floor in the back. Then I crouched under the window to the right of the door. The plan was that Sami would walk Heinz into the

166

shack, I would stick the gun into Heinz's back, and the good guys would win.

That was the plan, anyway.

I heard the car pull up and the car door open. Whoever it was didn't plan on being there long because he left the motor running.

Of course, I told myself, it was still possible that this wasn't Heinz but one of the legions of private eyes that Graham had doubtless sent to search for me. I mean, there had to be hundreds of white Land Rovers merrily off-roading the greater California-Nevada desert biome. It didn't have to be Heinz.

"Hello, Heinz!" Sami yelled.

Of course, it had to be Heinz. It had been that kind of "a errand." I resisted the urge to peek out the window as I heard footsteps coming our way. I did sneak a glance to Nathan.

He shrugged.

"Sami," Heinz said. "Where are—"

"In the shack," Sami said.

Very good, Sami. So far, so good.

"Heinz, they're in the shack and they have the gun!" Sami yelled.

Very bad, Sami. So far, so bad.

Sami having somewhat compromised the old element of surprise, I stood up and risked a peek out the window. Sami was bolting toward Heinz like a lost puppy toward his master. I could have indeed put one in his back except for three things: I'm a terrible shot with a pistol, I didn't have it in me, and Heinz had a forearm around Karen's throat and a gun to her head.

Talk about your element of surprise.

What the hell was she doing here? And what was Hope White doing in the passenger seat?

Using Karen as a shield, Heinz advanced toward the shack and yelled, "Put the gun down, Jew! Or I kill the girl!"

Did you ever wish you were Clint Eastwood? The issue of looks aside, did you ever wish you were Clint Eastwood so you could do the things he does in the movies?

See, Heinz was considerably taller than Karen so his whole big flat head was exposed. Clint Eastwood would have raised that old magnum and blown Heinz's head clear off his shoulders.

But I didn't feel that lucky. I really am a terrible shot and my hand was shaking anyway. I just didn't feel up to making a snap shot just above the head of the woman I love, the potential mother of my child.

"Drop the gun!" Heinz yelled. "Come out with your hands up!"

No kidding, he really said that.

And no kidding, I really did it. I couldn't think of anything else to do. I tossed the pistol out the window then stepped into the doorway.

I looked at Karen. She looked scared, of course, but by no means terrified.

"Hi," I said.

I don't do quips well in the face of danger.

"Hi," she answered. "How are you?"

"Oh, fine. How are you?"

"Ovulating."

How can you not want to make a baby with a woman who says things like that?

"Is the old Jew in there?" Heinz asked.

"What old Jew?" I answered.

"Nazi bastard!"

"I guess he is," I said.

"Then he's next," said Heinz. He smiled, raised the gun and pointed it right at my chest.

My heart stopped.

"Look out, sweetie!"

I hadn't even seen Hope slide into the driver's seat but now she was plowing straight toward Heinz's back.

Karen slipped out from under his arm and dove to the side. I flung myself sideways as the gun went off.

Twice.

I can't tell you what happened next. All I can tell you is that when the dust cleared—literally—the Land Rover was inside the shack, Karen was beating the crap out of Sami, and Heinz and I were on our hands and knees looking at each other.

And his gun was on the ground between us.

We went for each other instead of the gun. I was angry, and desperate to save Karen, whom I loved, and Nathan and Hope, whom I had come to like, and—to tell the truth—my own life. So I had a surge of adrenaline that I knew would carry me through. I knew I could take Heinz.

Because I had to.

He beat the hell out of me.

I almost went out when his first punch smashed into the side of my head. I punched back, though, and felt my fist smack into his jaw. I hit him three more times in the back of the neck before he lifted me over his shoulders and slammed me into the ground.

I thought my back was broken. I couldn't breathe and felt like there was a knife stabbing into my lungs. My eyes watered and I could barely see Heinz standing above me, grinning.

He pressed his boot onto my throat, leaned down, and started to pick up the gun.

Karen lunged for it.

Heinz whirled around and kicked her in the stomach. She doubled up and dropped to her knees.

I dove for the back of his legs and tackled him. I climbed up his back, got a forearm around his thick neck and started to choke him. The big son of a bitch got up, grabbed the back of my shirt and threw me over his shoulder. He held on to my hand, though, and as I flew through the air he twisted my arm and jerked.

I guess I screamed when my shoulder popped out of its socket.

I guess it was me. It might have been Karen, it might have been Hope, it could even have been Sami.

As I tried to get up I saw Sami grab the gun and hold it on Karen. I tried to push up with my feet but the ground was rolling around and the air was pressing down on my shoulders. It didn't help that I could see my shoulder muscle sitting like a lump in the vicinity of my elbow.

I aimed a punch at where I thought Heinz might be.

The next thing I saw was the flash of his boot in front of my face, and then the world went black.

Chapter 25

WHEN I STARTED TO COME TO, HEINZ WAS CARRY-
ing me on his shoulder like a sack of potatoes.

Which aptly described me: I was lumpy, bumpy, beat,
whipped, mashed, and about as useful in a fight.

So I was looking at the world upside-down and back-
ward as we headed up the dirt road up and behind the
opposite knoll.

I didn't much care, though. I was sick, dizzy and
hurting in body and soul. I was a miserable failure who
couldn't protect myself, the people I was supposed to
look out for, or the person I loved more than anyone in
the world.

Why Heinz hadn't done me the favor of just shooting
me back by the shack, I didn't know.

I was going to find out, because a few minutes later he
stopped and dropped me to the ground.

It took all of what little I had left to swallow the scream.

"*Ja,* this will do," I heard Heinz say.

He grabbed me under the arms and picked me up like a rag doll.

He stuck his face into my mine and said casually, "Sorry to do this, but I have only so many bullets, *ja*? And you made me waste two, so . . ."

A revolver. Six bullets; two fired, leaving four. Nathan, Hope, Sami and Karen.

"What . . ."

"Mine shaft," he said. "Boring hole. Fifty feet deep, perhaps. So you won't suffer long. And soon you have the company of your friends, *ja*?"

And he dropped me.

I slid down some dirt and then felt myself in open air. I fell and fell and waited for the smack at the bottom that should end this.

I didn't exactly smack.

I splashed.

I plunged feet-first underwater, didn't hit bottom, then struggled with my one good arm to the surface.

A circle of light tantalized about thirty feet up. The hole was about ten feet in circumference and God only knows how many scant desert rains it had taken to leave this much water.

I tried to grab the side and my hand slipped. I tried again. Same thing. I couldn't even feel my left hand, never mind raise it or grab anything. All I could do was tread water, and that just barely.

So there it is, I thought. There's no way out, no way to help the others, and nothing to do but tread water with one arm until I wear out. Nathan and Hope were beyond help, Karen would die, and I was drowning in the middle of the desert.

A while later, when I heard the distant, hollow thump of the shots, I decided that drowning wasn't so bad.

Chapter 26

MY RIBS HURT LIKE HELL AND MY HEART ACHED worse. As I watched Heinz-57 carry Neal away I knew I was never going to see him again.

Neal, I mean.

And yes, I started to cry. This time my heart really was broken and I didn't care that some little Arab midget was pointing a gun at me, and I didn't even care if he pulled the trigger.

My life was over anyway.

So when little . . . Sami, I guess his name was, herded Nathan and Hope out of what was left of the shack and sat us down in the sun to bake until Heinz-57 came to shoot us, I didn't much care.

That's the downside to loving someone. When they go they take so much of your life with them.

Anyway, old Heinz-57 came striding back a while later like he was King Shit, you know.

"What did you do to Neal?" I asked.

"Disposed of him," he said.

Then I really started crying. I didn't care that the son of a bitch was enjoying it. My damn heart was broken.

Heinz kept moving, fiddled with the Land Rover, and managed to back it out of the shack. Then he said to Sami, "You carry the old man's body, I carry this bitch. Then we come back. It will take both of us to carry the old lady."

"I beg your pardon!" Hope said.

"Okay," said Sami. "I—"

He stopped in his tracks. His mouth gaped as he looked over Heinz's shoulder. I looked too.

A Jeep was barreling in on us. The driver braked, the Jeep fishtailed and threw up a cloud of dust. When it cleared I saw an older, silver-haired man in an immaculate gray pinstripe suit climb easily out of the passenger side. The driver, a barrel-chested man in his early thirties, got out his own side.

Sami dropped his gun in the dirt. I could see Heinz holding his behind his back.

The silver-haired man said, "Hello, Mr. Silver."

Nathan said, "Good morning, Mr. C."

Mr. C turned to Heinz and said, "It's not polite to keep people sitting out in the sun like this. Particularly older people."

"What business is this of yours?" Heinz asked.

"Where's Neal Carey?"

I couldn't see Heinz-57's face, but I knew it had that arrogant smirk on it as he said, "The same place you'll—"

He swung out the gun and went into a macho-man combat crouch.

I swear that Mr. C didn't move, flinch, or even blink as his driver pulled his own gun and shot Heinz-57 four times in the chest before Heinz could even raise his pistol. Mr. C just turned his gaze to Sami and asked, "Where's Neal Carey?"

Sami's hand shook as he pointed toward the opposite hill.

I got up and ran.

Chapter 27

I DON'T KNOW HOW LONG IT WAS BEFORE I HEARD the footsteps.

At first they seemed far off and muffled and I didn't yell because it didn't matter anymore. I figured that it was Heinz and Sami and that they were about to drop the bodies down the shaft. I didn't want to see that anyway so I closed my eyes and tried to drown.

Then I heard someone say, "I don't know, ma'am. I'm afraid he's dead."

And Karen say, "Then I want to find his body!"

Karen? "His body"?

"Down here!" I yelled. "I'm down here!"

I could hear the footsteps shuffling around.

"DOWN HERE! I'M DOWN HERE!"

"NEAL?!"

"DOWN HERE! DOWN HERE!"

I saw Karen's face peek out from the circle of blue sky.

"Hold on, babe!" she shouted. "They're bringing a rope!"

"Are you okay?!"

"I think I have a cracked rib! Are you okay!?"

"Well, I'm alive!"

"Well I guess that beats the alternative!" she hollered. "I love you!"

"I love you, too!"

"Nathan?!" I asked.

"He's okay!"

"Hope?!"

"Fine!" she yelled. "Everyone's fine except for Heinz-57! I don't think he's going to make it!"

Actually, I didn't care if Heinz made it or not.

"You hang in there, babe!" Karen yelled. "They're coming!"

They came a few minutes later. I saw the rope come down and managed to grab the end with my right hand. Then I saw the barrel-chested guy from the Sands peer over the edge.

"Can you loop that around yourself and tie it off?" he asked.

I didn't want to say that I probably couldn't do that standing on dry ground with two good arms, so I yelled, "I can try!"

"Trying won't cut it!" he yelled. He pulled the rope back up. "Hold on."

A few minutes later he was in the water with me. He

looped the rope around both of us and yelled, "Take her up!"

I could hear the Jeep moaning in the sand. A minute later we were in daylight.

At first the sun blinded me so I couldn't see Karen. I could *feel* her, though, as she put her arms around me. When I was able to see her face, there were tears on her cheeks.

I wanted to cry too, to be honest. But Mickey the C was standing there in a three-piece suit, in the desert sun, not even sweating. Not a bead of perspiration on his smooth face.

"Thank you," I said.

"No problem," he answered. "Anything for Natty Silver, the laughs he's given me. And Joe Graham reached out for you. Said you're like a son to him."

Okay, maybe then my eyes might have moistened a little bit.

Don't ever tell Graham, though, okay?

In the distance I heard the basslike beating of helicopter rotors.

"The cops?" I asked.

Mickey the C snorted. "The cops? They take forever to get here."

A few minutes later I was on a stretcher beside Nathan Silver on a mob helicopter zooming us back to Las Vegas.

We'd been in the air about ten seconds when he mumbled, "So Arthur Minsky says to the Irish kid, 'Son, you're never going to be a good errand boy. Can you do anything else?' And the kid, Costello, says, 'I want to be a comic.' Arthur laughs, I laugh, Eileen the Irish Dream laughs, Benny the Blade laughs. Then Arthur turns to me and says, 'There you go, Natty. Here's your replacement for Phil Gold. Teach *him* "Who's on First." ' And I say, 'This kid? He can't learn it. He's the dumbest Mick I ever seen! Dumber maybe than you, even.' I said to Arthur Minsky . . ."

"Nathan?"

"Yeeees?"

"Didn't I meet you in Cleveland once?"

"I've never been to Cleveland."

"Neither have I," I said. "Must have been two other guys."

And I actually got a laugh out of Natty Silver.

Chapter 28

Ms. Pamela A. Holmstrum
Claims Superintendent
Western States Insurance Co.
801 Flower Street
Los Angeles, CA

Craig D. Schaeffer
Attorney-at-Law
3615 Monterey
Palm Desert, CA

14 August 1983

Dear Mr. Schaeffer,

Congratulations on your fine work on the Muller-Abdullah files. I was gratified to receive your communication that Attorney Eugene Petkovitch has dropped both bad-faith suits. Of course, I imagine that Mr. Muller's demise and Mr. Abdullah's incarceration rendered that litigation moot.

Western States Insurance Company is very pleased with your fine work on this file, and please allow me to add my personal congratulations. It has been a pleasure to work with you and I look forward to future collaborations.

Yours truly,
Pamela A. Holmstrum

P.S.: See, I told you things would work out.

>))

Craig D. Schaeffer
Attorney-at-Law
3615 Monterey
Palm Desert, CA

Ms. Pamela A. Holmstrum
Claims Superintendent
Western States Insurance Co.
801 Flower Street
Los Angeles, CA

17 August 1983

Dear Ms. Holmstrum,

Thank you for your letter expressing your, and your company's, appreciation for my modest efforts on the Muller-Abdullah file. I am indeed gratified that everything worked out. Let me also express my appreciation for your work on the matter and say how much I have enjoyed our association. I hope it will continue.

Sincerely,
Craig Schaeffer, Esquire

P.S.: Dinner Saturday?

❯ ❯ ❯

Ms. Pamela A. Holmstrum
Claims Superintendent
Western States Insurance Co.
801 Flower Street
Los Angeles, CA

Craig D. Schaeffer
Attorney-at-Law
3615 Monterey
Palm Desert, CA

19 August 1983

Dear Craig,
    Please find enclosed a correspondence from Eugene Petkovitch. I am referring this to you for your handling.

Yours truly,
Pam Holmstrum

P.S.: Do you believe the nerve of this son-of-a-gun?

P.P.S.: Eight o'clock?

The Law Offices of Eugene E. Petkovitch
1500 Mitch Miller Boulevard
Palm Springs, CA

Ms. Pamela Holmstrum
Western States Insurance Co.
801 Flower Street
Los Angeles, CA

16 August 1983

Dear Ms. Holmstrum,
   This letter is to inform you that I no longer
represent Mr. Amin "Sami" Abdullah. If I had
thought for a moment that this man was an arsonist,
fraud and kidnapper I would never have deigned to
take pen in hand—rhetorically speaking—on his
behalf. Please accept my profound apologies.
   Second, I wish to inform you that I will be filing
suit against you on behalf of the estate of the late
Heinz Muller. The causes of action will be unlawful
surveillance, harassment, assault with a deadly
vehicle (his Land Rover) false imprisonment, and
wrongful death. I am also naming Mr. Neal Carey,
Mr. Nathan Silverstein, Ms. Hope White, Ms. Karen
Hawley, and one John Doe aka "Mickey the C."
   I am personally and professionally outraged—
OUTRAGED—that an insurance carrier in this day
and age would single out for oppressive treatment
an individual just because that person happens to be
a foreign immigrant. Immigration built this land,

Ms. Holmstrum, lest you or Western States Insurance Company ever forget it!

Your conduct has been despicable!

I am certain that a California jury will send a message to the insurance industry—via a large punitive damages award—that this type of conduct will no longer be tolerated.

There is still time for you to avoid litigation.

My client, the estate of Mr. Heinz Muller, is generously willing to accept $100,000,000 for the pain, suffering and unlawful death that your Gestapo-like inquisition and jackboot investigative tactics have inflicted upon him. This sum represents far less than an outraged jury would award, and saves you the cost of a long, expensive, and ultimately futile defense.

This offer expires at close of business, five working days hence, and will not be compromised or renewed.

Sincerely yours,
Eugene E. Petkovitch

❯   ❯   ❯

Craig D. Schaeffer
Attorney-at-Law
3615 Monterey
Palm Desert, CA

Ms. Pamela A. Holmstrum
Claims Superintendent
Western States Insurance Co.
801 Flower Street
Los Angeles, CA

20 August 1983

Dear Pam,

Enclosed please find my response to the demand letter of Attorney Eugene Petkovitch.

Here we go again.

Sincerely,
Craig

P.S.: Enjoyed watching *The Searchers.* Was it John Wayne, or you?

〉   〉   〉

Craig D. Schaeffer
Attorney-at-Law
3615 Monterey
Palm Desert, CA

Eugene E. Petkovitch
The Law Offices of Eugene E. Petkovitch
1500 Mitch Miller Boulevard
Palm Springs, CA

20 August 1983

Dear Eugene,

I am once again representing Western States Insurance Company. In response to your latest correspondence:

1) Take us to court.
2) Bring your lunch.

The usual bullshit,
Craig "Mad Dog" Schaeffer

⟩ ⟩ ⟩

By Fax

Dear Craig,

I read with great interest your response to Attorney Petkovitch.

I have a triathlon in Laguna next weekend. Can you lend me some testosterone?

Pam

P.S.: I rented Annie Hall, if that will get you here.

Chapter 29

Dear Diary,

What a day!

I went over to visit Nathan in the hospital. He is sharing a room with that nice young man Neal. Nathan says Neal is kind of grumpy sometimes but Nathan puts up with it because he says that Neal is very eager to learn all about the good old days in burlesque so Nathan is telling him all about it.

Nathan is feeling much better even though the ordeal was very hard on him. He has decided to buy a condo here in Las Vegas. At first, Diary, he wanted to move in with me but I didn't think that would be proper. So I told him to get his own place nearby and I would come over for matinees (blush, blush).

That nice young man Neal is also recovering. He had a dislocated shoulder, a cracked cheekbone, a bruised hip, a bruised throat, a concussion and multiple contusions. He says he is eager to get out of the hospital. In fact the other day, right in the middle of one of Nathan's lessons about burlesque, Neal said that if he didn't get out of the room soon he was going to stick his head down the commode and try to flush himself. I think he must have been joking, though, because they won't let him up to use the bathroom and I think he is a little jealous of Nathan about this. Nathan is already in a wheelchair and Neal is still in bed.

I'm sure he was happy to see his fiancée, Karen. You remember, Diary, the nice girl that Neal would not get in a family way? She came in today as usual, but she had a special gleam in her eye, if you know what I mean (blush, blush). She came in and said hello to us and kissed Neal on the cheek.

"How are you?" she asked.

"Better," he said.

"Headache?"

"No."

"Shoulder?"

"Not bad."

She smiled and dug into her purse. Then she pulled out a twenty-dollar bill and slipped it to me. "Sweetie," she whispered, "can I treat you to a movie or something?"

She winked at me and I winked back and then I rolled Nathan down to the cafeteria. They have slot machines there.

Karen was pulling the curtain around Neal's bed as we left. I don't know what went on in that room while we were gone, Diary! (Blush, blush.)

Your confidante,

Hope

Chapter 30

MEN ARE DEPENDABLE, GOD BLESS 'EM. YOU CAN bust them up, throw them down a mine shaft, and half drown them . . . they can have broken bones, a cracked head, and a body that's one big bruise . . . in short, they can just hurt all over, and if that *one part* works they still want to, you know, *do it.*

It's just one of the things I love about them.

Not that I jumped right into the sack. ("Eased" is more like it, anyway. When the moment came I "eased" into the sack, Neal being in a delicate condition and all.) First we made a little small talk.

"Petkovitch is suing you?!" I asked when Neal told me.

"He's suing you, too."

"That's outrageous," I said. "Do you know a good lawyer?"

"I don't think we'll be needing one," Neal answered. "He's also suing Mickey the C."

"That's not real bright."

"It's downright dim," Neal said. "Mickey the C's idea of playing rough includes a little more than sarcastic remarks in his correspondence."

"I noticed."

"Right."

"So how are you?" I asked.

"I hurt all over."

"One big bruise."

"One big bruise."

"I gave Hope twenty bucks."

"What for?" he asked.

"Get rid of her."

"And Nathan?"

"And Nathan."

"What for?"

Giving me that innocent look as if he didn't have a clue.

"Never mind," I said. "You're in pain."

"Actually, I'm starting to feel better."

"And you need your rest."

"In moderation," he said. "With exercise."

"But you can't get out of bed."

"Nope."

"Nope."

"So any exercise you're going to get . . ."

". . . would have to be in bed."

"Hmmm."

"Hmmm."

I shut and locked the door, then got out of my clothes.

"I'm really feeling considerable improvement," Neal said.

What can I tell you? The guy makes me laugh.

"It must be the tender, loving care," I said.

"Is that it?"

"It's about to be."

Then I eased into the bed.

Epilogue

KAREN WAS JUST GETTING OUT OF THE SHOWER when I asked her to get me a Diet Pepsi.

"Excuse me?" she murmured.

"I'm in postcoital bliss," I said. "And when I'm in postcoital bliss I need a Diet Pepsi."

"Why don't you get one?"

I shook my head.

"When a man's in postcoital bliss it's the woman's job to get the Diet Pepsi," I smiled. "Besides, I'm not supposed to get out of bed."

"I'm in postcoital bliss, too."

"Too bad."

I looked at her with what I liked to think was a lascivious expression.

"Besides," I said, "it's your fault."

She got dressed and went out to the little refrigerator in the hall to get me a Diet Pepsi.

The phone rang.

"Hello, son."

"Hello, Dad."

"What's this I got in the mail today?" he asked.

"From me?"

"No, from Elvis," he said. "Yes, from you."

"It's a Father's Day card," I answered.

"It isn't Father's Day," Graham said.

"It should be," I said.

There was a long silence over the phone. Then I said, "Dad, thanks for finding me."

"Forget it," Graham said. "So how's Palm Springs?"

I laughed, then he nagged me about my various terrible injuries and I told him I was okay.

"Well, you take care of yourself," he said.

"Yeah, you too."

We would have gone on in that vein but it would have been absolutely bathetic.

Karen came back in, sat down on the bed and handed me the Diet Pepsi.

"Did we attempt to make a baby?" I asked.

I was willing. I thought I could handle it.

Talk about your long silences.

Then she shook her head.

"I still want to, though," she said.

"I think I do, too."

"But you don't *know*," she said.

"No."

She sighed, lay down next to me in the bed, and snuggled her face into my neck.

"Not knowing's not good enough," she said.

"I'm sorry."

"Don't be sorry. Wherever you go, there you are."

We held each other as tightly as two people with various broken bones could.

"I think you're right," I said. "I think I have a lot of stuff to work out."

"I hate saying it," she said. "But I think so, too. I just want you to *know*. I've been thinking about it, too. A kid deserves that, you know?"

"Yeah, I do."

"I guess you do."

I swallowed hard and said, "So I think I'll go see somebody."

"You mean like a shrink?"

"Don't sound so shocked."

"No, I think it's good idea," she said. "I'm just surprised that you do."

"I don't. I just don't know how else to go about it."

We shared some more silence.

"I think we should postpone the wedding," she said.

"Is that a gentle way of saying we're not getting married?"

"No, it's a gentle way of saying that we shouldn't get married until we know what we want," she said. "And I guess we need to be alone for a while."

That scared the shit out of me.

"You'll be there when I come back?"

"If it works out that way," she said. "And I hope it works out that way. I love you."

"I love you, too."

> > >

I left the hospital two days later. I was still sore and still hurting and had a heroic limp, but it was time to go. I said good-bye to Nathan and Hope. Karen had already left.

Saying goodbye to Nathan was harder than I thought it would be. It's funny—first I couldn't wait to get rid of him, and when I finally did I felt kind of sad. I just had this feeling that I had seen the last of Natty Silver and that there weren't any more coming down the road.

I don't want to talk about saying good-bye to Karen.

I didn't really know where I was going so I finally got on that flight to Palm Springs. I hated to leave a trip unfinished, I wanted to find a shrink, and I figured that they probably had a few of them in California.

So I never should have got out of the hot tub, right? Sometimes you get out of the hot water just to jump right back into it.

But maybe you have to almost drown before you really learn to swim. And sometimes you find out that you're somewhat broken and you can't swim at all.

But you do anyway.

Drowning in the desert, you just tread water.

CARMEL CLAY PUBLIC LIBRARY
515 E. Main St.
Carmel, IN 46032
(317) 844-3361

1. This item is due on the latest date stamped on the card above.

2. A fine shall be paid on each item which is not returned according to Library policy. No item may be borrowed by the person incurring the fine until it is paid.

3. Any resident of Clay Township,complying with Library regulations, may borrow materials

DEMCO